IDIOTS

FIVE FAIRY TALES *and* OTHER STORIES

JAKOB ARJOUNI

IDIOTS

FIVE FAIRY TALES *and* OTHER STORIES

Translated from the German
by *Anthea Bell*

Other Press · New York

The publication of this work was supported by a grant from the Goethe-Institut.

Ein Freund: copyright © 1998 by Diogenes Verlag AG, Zurich, Switzerland
Idioten. Fünf Märchen: © 2003 by Diogenes Verlag AG, Zurich, Switzerland
Translation copyright © 2005 Anthea Bell

Production Editor: Robert D. Hack
Text design: Natalya Balvova
This book was set in 10.2 pt Janson Text by Alpha Graphics, Pittsfield, NH.

10 9 8 7 6 5 4 3 2 1

Library of Congress Cataloging-in-Publication Data

Arjouni, Jakob.
  [Idioten. English]
  Idiots : five fairy tales and other stories / by Jakob Arjouni ; translated from the German by Anthea Bell.
    p. cm.
  ISBN 1-59051-157-3 (hardcover : alk. paper)
  I. Bell, Anthea.   II. Title.
  PT2661.R45I3613 2005
  833'.914–dc22   2004022638

for Miranda

CONTENTS

IDIOTS

When the fairy visited Max he was sitting outside Rico's Sports Bar in Berlin on a warm spring evening, drinking beer and thinking: the trouble with idiots is, they're too idiotic to see their own idiocy. He was meeting Ronnie for a meal an hour from now, and if he didn't finally have it out with Ronnie then who would? Because opinion in the office was unanimous: not only was Ronnie acting to most of the staff like the ultimate bastard, if he carried on running the agency the way he'd been doing these last few months he'd lose them all their jobs. Only this morning he'd brought off two more masterstrokes: first he'd canceled Nina's vacation with her new boyfriend, which was already booked and paid for, because apparently he absolutely needed her around for a particular campaign and her only alternative was to be fired. Then he sent out a press release saying the Good Reasons advertising agency had acquired the services of world-famous photographer Eliot Barnes as a permanent member of staff, even though there'd been only a couple of informal discussions with him to date, nothing definite. Before three hours were up Barnes's agent called. She was ruling out any more collaboration with him until further notice. Max, whom Ronnie sent out in such cases as a firefighter to retrieve the situation, had spent all afternoon phoning several of Barnes's colleagues, Barnes's agent, and finally Barnes in person, explaining over and over again that the press release had been written, in a moment of what was obviously slightly deranged wishful thinking, by a trainee on work experience who was an enthusiastic fan of Barnes's work. Apart from Barnes himself, who seemed to feel that a fan's enthusiasm for his work was a plausible reason for practically anything, everyone indicated first that the tale of the trainee on work experience didn't sound particularly credible, and second that there really did seem to be something in the rumors that, ever since Good Reasons was launched on the stock exchange, it kept publishing half-truths about its big contracts and the deals it had done, just to keep the stockholders sweet.

Max shook his head. Oh, brilliant move! How the hell did Ronnie think he was going to get away with such a dumb notion?

When Ronnie had founded Good Reasons eight years ago, with Max as his first employee and still more or less an equal partner in the outfit, their idea had been to publicize exclusively products and institutions that they felt were doing good to the world and humanity: Amnesty International, Bread for the World, Greenpeace, coffee direct from the producing countries, organic products, antiracist campaigns, nonprofit-making enterprises. But in spite of their copious self-promotion in newspaper ads and selectively mailed circulars, no one showed any interest in them at first, not Greenpeace, or the coffee-growing countries, or anyone else with a name that sounded good and some financial muscle, only a few apple growers from Brandenburg and a Dutch bicycle-repair firm in Kreuzberg. After a year in which they had done little more, as Ronnie put it, than "print lousy sunrises with pothead texts, looking all smudged and hand-made, on kind of A4 toilet paper," because their clients couldn't be induced to pay for anything else, they decided that for the time being they'd also work for firms whose business might not be doing the world quite as much good. First a jewelry store on the Kudamm, then a couple of fashion boutiques, finally a firm selling furniture made from exotic woods over the Internet. There'd been some initial debate about this firm. After all, it wasn't easy to reconcile the philosophy of Good Reasons with the despoliation of rain forests. But the agency was on the point of going bust, and the furniture firm wanted a countrywide campaign.

So one thing led to another. The campaign for the furniture firm was a huge success, other firms hired Good Reasons to publicize yogurt, sparkling wines, cell phones, men's suits, and when a motor company known to make a large part of its money from tanks got in touch a year later, their slightly embarrassed hesitation lasted barely an afternoon before the champagne corks popped. Four years after that, Good Reasons was one of the three or four most powerful and profitable advertising agencies in Germany. Ronnie had long ago become its undisputed boss, and Max was just his willing right-hand man, so his attempts to persuade Ronnie not to go public on the stock exchange didn't carry much weight.

"Christ, Max, we've been working our socks off for years, and where has it got us? Do you have a lakeside villa? Do I have a lakeside villa? Right now we're doing better than ever, and here's our one and only chance to make a real killing."

"Suppose we stop doing so well?"

"Oh, for God's sake! If you had your way we'd still be advertising rotten apples for some kind of hippies. The world's our oyster—that's the way you want to see it."

"All I see is a couple of firms giving us pretty good contracts right now."

"And what do you think they'll do when we've gone public? They'll buy Good Reasons stock and give us twice as many contracts."

"Could be."

"Oh, Max, Max, Max, Max—little Max! Where would you be without me?"

"Hm. And another thing: if you remember, there's still our old Good Reasons memo of association. I don't suppose you're going to float the agency on the stock exchange with that."

"Oh, that old thing—chuck it out."

"Still, it mightn't be a bad idea to have some explanation of why we thought the name up. Just for our image."

"Good Reasons? I don't need any explanation for the name. And once they have to show that funny chart of theirs rising because of our stock prices . . ." Ronnie grinned so widely that Max could see his molars, ". . . well, then at least it'll show what good reasons we have."

And so a year ago they did it: Good Reasons was listed on the stock exchange. Rates did rise during the first few months, stayed at a good level for a while, and then crashed during the crisis on the new market. Today their stocks were worth only a fifth of the original listing price. And instead of bringing in new clients as before with his expansive go-getting charm, giving off an aura of optimism, building all kinds of castles in the air, sketching fantastic visions of collaboration, Ronnie now had to listen to every publicity budget manager pointing out that the Good Reasons stock was at rock bottom, so his visions clearly weren't worth much.

Max finished his beer, turned around in his chair and waved a hand back at the Sports Bar to order another. Just then Sophie turned the corner of the building. Their eyes met and Sophie slowed down, as if she felt like turning back. Then she quickened her pace again, came up to Max's table and said in friendly tones, "Hi, Max. Knocked off work for the day?"

"Just a break, I'm afraid. I'm meeting Ronnie."

"Ah. I see."

As usual, Max found it hard to interpret Sophie's expression.

"Did you hear what he said to Nina this morning?" she asked.

"Yes, what a mess."

"You think so?"

"Of course I think so. Even if . . . look, he's anxious about the firm, that's what it is, and Nina's the very best at her job."

"So why does he threaten to fire her if she takes the vacation she told him about two months back?"

"Well, you know how Ronnie sometimes is. I mean, whether he'd really fire her . . ."

"You bet I know how Ronnie sometimes is. So I told Nina she'd better wave good-bye to that vacation if she wants to keep her job."

Max moved his head slightly back and forth, gazed at the table in front of him, and said earnestly, "Look, I think you're exaggerating. I mean, one can discuss anything with Ronnie."

"Oh yes? Then you discuss it with him."

Max would have liked to say that was exactly what he planned to do this evening, and he was going to make things very clear. But then maybe tomorrow Sophie would ask him what came of the discussion, and maybe nothing would have come of it, and he always felt somehow useless when he was talking to Sophie anyway.

"I'll have a word with Nina tomorrow first. Maybe she can put her vacation off for a couple of weeks. Of course the agency would shoulder the extra expense."

"Of course."

"Oh, come on. We did that before, right? With Roger last year."

"As far as I know you gave Roger the money out of your own pocket."

Max opened his mouth and for a moment he looked the way he hated to look, particularly in front of Sophie—like totally useless. And how could she have known? The question was burning in his head.

"It was only an advance. I got the money back when we worked out the expenses, of course."

"Of course."

"Well, what did you think?"

"I thought Ronnie was telling the truth around the end of the Christmas party, when he was drunk as a skunk and laughing his head off at you. He didn't have to do a thing to keep the staff happy, he said, little Max saw to all that, he'd even throw his own salary away on third-rate staff members so they could go off surfing and not bear Good Reasons a grudge."

Max ground his teeth and stuck out his lips, looking both insulted and furious.

"That's not true."

"What's not true? That Ronnie would say such a thing or that you paid the money out of your own pocket?"

"I got it back."

"Well, maybe he didn't know."

"After the Christmas party."

"I see. So you're in a position to catch up on expenses even a year later."

"Exactly. Anyway, Ronnie and I've known each other so long and so well we can always have a good laugh at one another. We don't have any problems with that."

"Hm. And you yourself specially enjoy having a good laugh at Ronnie."

"I don't think you've seen me in private often enough to judge."

"No, unfortunately not."

Suddenly Max couldn't think of anything else to say. Sophie simply stood there. He was about to pick up his beer glass, but just in time he remembered that it was empty.

"Oh well," said Sophie at last. "Have a nice evening."

"You too," replied Max. "See you tomorrow."

After Sophie had disappeared past a line of parked cars, it took Max some time to convince himself that their conversation had been only ironic banter between two determined characters. Then he waved back at the bar behind him again.

He was still waving when he saw a movement out of the corner of his eye. He turned his head, and there was the fairy, hovering in front of him.

"Good evening," said the fairy.

"Good evening," replied Max, leaving his arm vertical in the air as a sign to the waiter, and expecting her to ask him for directions to somewhere, or a cigarette. He did notice that the figure in front of him seemed somehow transparent, with bare feet that didn't touch the ground, but he put that down to the style of her shimmering sky-blue dress and the effect of a pair of cleverly made sandals. Maybe she worked in fashion. There were a couple of little studios not far from the Sports Bar.

"I am a fairy and I've come to grant you a wish."

Max had been looking back at the doorway again, hoping that a thirsty glance would catch the eye of the waiter, who obviously hadn't noticed his outstretched arm. So it took some time for the fairy's words to sink in.

"What did you say?"

"I'm a fairy," repeated the fairy, "and I've come to grant you a wish."

Max looked confused at first, then he dropped his arm and frowned suspiciously. Was this some kind of joke? An ad, maybe? The Schultheiss Good Fairy, or the Marlboro Good Fairy, promising men sitting around on their own a wish, their choice of a mountain bike or a knife collection if they ordered ten packs of cigarettes or two crates of beer every week for a year? Or was it one of those TV gags? But then where were the cameras? Or was she just a nut case?

"Listen, if this is some kind of game . . ."

"No. I'm a real fairy, and you really can have one wish granted. The following areas are out, though: immortality, health, money, love," said the fairy, reeling off her patter. This was her tenth date of the day, maybe her thousandth since the boss promoted her from shooting-star service to the inner circle of fairies. She'd seen every kind of amazement and heard every kind of question, although in muted form, because to give the fairies enough time to grant wishes without having to explain at length, on every occasion, exactly who they were and what they could do, something about their aura kept the lucky recipients of their attentions from expressing more than a relatively slight degree of surprise, alarm, inquiry, or doubt. From the moment of her appearance a fairy's visit seemed to most people almost as normal as a date with a car mechanic or a tax adviser, not many of whose customers really understood their professional utterances fully, and while a number of ways of getting a car through inspection or a profit past the Internal Revenue Service might seem to outsiders to border on magic, few insisted on understanding every detail of a process that was obviously to their advantage.

Max hesitated for a moment, listened to the echo of the fairy's words, tried to get his mind around their meaning, shook his head, glanced around briefly to see if the world was still the same, and then leaned across the table. "You really are hovering in the air, right?"

"Yes, we all do."

"You all do? You mean there are several fairies?"

"Oh, no end of us. Even so, we can hardly keep up with our schedules. People just make too many wishes."

Max nodded hesitantly, leaned back again, and reached blindly for his cigarettes. "You mean you have to go anywhere someone wishes for something?"

"That's about it. But like I said, we can hardly keep up, and quite often we're too late."

Without taking his eyes off the fairy, Max lit a cigarette. He could see the façade of the building opposite and a pharmacist's sign through the fairy's thin, nondescript, rather weary face. Max felt his mouth go dry. He wasn't normally the sort to be impressed by any kind of hocus-pocus. It was true that he avoided gypsy fortune tellers, he'd learned in Russia that you shouldn't drink a toast with alcohol-free beverages, and he sometimes touched wood when he was thinking about death and sickness. But he didn't believe in any God except his own, and he was convinced there was a logical explanation for everything in the world if you only thought about it long enough and used your brain. The dice fell the way you threw them, and that was it. (And he suspected that he didn't always throw his own dice very cleverly.)

But this was clearly something quite different. He'd drunk only a single glass of beer so far, and if he banged his knee on the table leg he could feel it. All the same, here was this transparent figure hovering in front of him and offering him a wish. And he thought she was telling the truth.

"What did I wish for, then?"

"Sorry. I hear so many wishes I often can't remember them separately."

"But I probably wish for something every day."

"That makes no difference. One of your wishes brought me here. So now you can wish for whatever you want—within the rules, of course."

"Ah." Whatever I want, thought Max, looking perplexed. "Which areas were out again?"

"Immortality, health, money, love."

Max drew on the cigarette and shook his head thoughtfully. He could have thought of a love wish straightaway. For instance, he'd been meeting Rosalie from the toothpaste ad regularly for the last two months to play badminton, and he'd never gotten further than a quick kiss on the cheek. He'd wondered whether she might be a lesbian. And then, like anyone else, he longed for the great, deep, enduring love that seemed to be retreating ever further from him with experience and the years. Money wishes would have been quick to think up too. It was true he didn't earn a bad salary, but he'd put all his savings into Good Reasons stock out of loyalty to Ronnie. The lakeside villa foretold by Ronnie as the result of being listed on the stock exchange had seemed further beyond his means than ever these last six years. (He preferred not to let his mind dwell too much on the fact that a villa—a twelve-roomed villa with a little park and its own landing stage—had proved to be within Ronnie's means four months after they were listed.) And how about health and immortality? Max was in his mid-thirties, and in spite of the cigarettes and booze the doctor assured him every few years that he was in the best of health. Of course now that he'd passed his thirtieth birthday he did sometimes find himself counting. If things turned out badly his life was half over, and Max liked life. He wouldn't have minded a few extra years. But what would they be worth without good health? Suppose he wished to live to be a hundred, and then he was bedridden from the age of seventy? Fed through a tube or something?

Max tossed his cigarette end away and looked back at the fairy, who had begun hovering on the spot a little impatiently. "What do other people wish for?"

"Oh, all kinds of things. Lots of them want a couple of weeks' vacation. Others want a dishwasher."

"A dishwasher?" Max looked astonished. "You can't be serious!"

"Yes, I am. Dishwashers come close to the top of the list. Third or fourth place."

"What's in first place?"

"Being famous."

"Oh . . . and how do you fix that every time if so many people want it?"

"Guess."

"No idea."

"Talk shows." Max thought he saw a chilly smile flit across the fairy's lips. "The fact is, it's our doing that there's so many of them on TV these days. Our boss thought up the idea."

"You mean your boss decides exactly how a wish is granted?"

"If it's not clearly defined. Which happens quite often with wanting to be famous. If you ask famous for what, or why, not many people know, but they still stick to their wish. Then it's up to the boss."

"I don't call a talk show a very attractive idea."

"But it works, and anyway it's more attractive than making other people jump off skyscrapers."

"Well, if you look at it that way . . . but doesn't being famous really come under the heading of immortality? And a dishwasher under the heading of money?"

"Oh, think about it long enough and I guess every wish comes under one of those headings."

"It doesn't take much thinking to work out that a dishwasher costs money."

The fairy sighed. "Listen, I didn't make the rules. I'm on the receiving end of wishes, I tell people what they can have and what they can't. A dishwasher is okay, a thousand marks isn't. If you want to know why you'd have to ask the boss."

"Can people do that?"

"In certain cases, yes, he deals with the wishes himself. Wishes about really important things: revolutions, wars, famines, inoculations, inventions."

Famines, inoculations . . . Max remembered how he and Ronnie had spent nights on end eight years ago, drawing up a charity campaign for crisis-stricken areas. And they'd done it without the usual photos of dying children and dried-up river beds, they'd done it with snapshots of Berlin high society pigging out and boozing in expensive restaurants. A newspaper editor with a bit of schnitzel hanging out of his fat face, and a caption under it saying: *If you don't buy his rag for a week he won't starve—and the money you aren't spending can save a human life in Ethiopia*. Or the theatrical impresario sitting in front of a row of empty champagne bottles arm in arm with the Senator for Culture: *His next ten flops will make him money even without the price of your ticket—so send that fifty marks and help a family to survive.*

But the charity organizations who were offered the campaign thought it too aggressive. If the fairy had come to see me then, thought Max, I could have wished they'd buy the campaign and it would succeed. But today . . . ?

It confused Max to think you could wish something about famines. As if someone had reminded him of the ideals of his youth—and a feeling of shame arose in him. Could he think of a wish to make for starving people today? He didn't even know exactly where they were now. Still in Ethiopia? Or could he just wish for no one to starve anymore? But that was silly. Someone else would surely have tried it long before him, and obviously it didn't work. It probably came under the heading of health. Or money.

While Max was thinking, his sense of shame grew stronger and stronger. As if he knew that in the end, if he did make a more personal wish after all, as was clearly expected, his thoughts were only to help him not seem too selfish to himself. Because thinking about the hunger in the world was almost like doing something about it. Being aware of a problem, after all, was the first step to solving it. And how many people simply ignored the plight of the starving? So that left him occupying the moral high ground. All the same, he couldn't entirely fool himself that way.

And then he suddenly had an idea. Suppose he suggested to Ronnie starting something up on the old Good

Reasons basis again? As a nonprofit-making sideline? Wouldn't that in itself be a fantastic ad? He could see the headlines in the business sections of the papers: *Giant Ad Agency Mounts Free Campaign for Bread for the World*. Or: *Good Reasons Leads the Way—for Genuinely Good Reasons*. Wouldn't that send their stock prices soaring at once?

Max was still picturing Ronnie's appreciative grin and the grateful faces of the Bread for the World bosses when the fairy cleared her throat slightly and said, "Excuse me, but I do have several more deadlines today, and time is getting on . . ."

Max sat up. "Yes, sure." He reached for his cigarettes. "How about a lakeside villa?"

The fairy looked surprised for a moment. Perhaps she'd expected something less ordinary after all the time he'd spent thinking. Then she shook her head. "Too expensive."

"But it's not money. I mean, it's like with the dishwasher." Max began stammering. Just now he'd had it all perfectly worked out: he was going to save the firm, and at the same time do something toward saving the world, so he could wish with a clear conscience for what he really wanted, and he thought he'd earned it too.

"There's a price difference. We're allowed a certain amount of latitude with wishes for material things. Lakeside villas are way beyond it."

Max's face showed first disappointment, then anger. He had noticed the fairy's surprised look, and for a moment he saw himself through her eyes. A lakeside villa! How crude could you get?

Pretending to be slightly amused, he hastily explained, "I just wanted to know what's possible and what isn't. I didn't really mean that wish seriously."

"Right," said the fairy, "so could we get to the one you do mean seriously?"

"Okay." Max was about to put the cigarette he had been holding for a few minutes between his lips when he noticed that the tobacco was falling out of the damp, splitting paper. As he threw the cigarette away, wiped and picked the tobacco crumbs off his perspiring hand, and finally took a new one, it seemed to him he could feel the fairy's glance following every movement he made, and instead of coming up with a wish he thought only of her opinion of him and what it might be.

"Don't make such heavy weather of it," said the fairy, seeing Max's hand tremble slightly as he struck a match. "There's no such thing as one great, perfect wish."

Max looked up at her thankfully. "But people try to find it, right? And when you mentioned revolutions and famines just now, it suddenly looked like I had a chance to change the world."

The fairy shook her head. "You don't. No one does. If you knew where and when rain was needed, you could wish for it. Not long ago someone wished for meat for North Korea, and that gave the boss the idea of the mad cow disease scare and having the Europeans send their sick cattle over there."

"But that's. . . ." Max just stopped himself from looking too horrified. He didn't want to play the moralist so soon after wishing for a lakeside villa—but all the same!

"Yes?"

"Well, I mean, that's not very nice."

"No one said the way we grant wishes is always nice. But I can assure you the meat satisfied people's hunger, which after all was the idea. Could you please get to your wish now?"

Max hesitated, as if he had something on the tip of his tongue, but then he just said, "Sure, in a minute," and tried to concentrate. However, Max had never been the sort who shone in exams.

"Think of ordinary everyday things. They're usually much simpler and more satisfying. Only yesterday someone wished not to feel any pain when his wisdom teeth were extracted, and I tell you, when I flew in for a moment that afternoon to see if he was okay, I found one of my happiest customers of the last few weeks."

Max nodded abstractedly. His head seemed to be getting emptier every second, but the words "a wish, a wish!" kept hammering away in the background. For a moment he had seriously wondered whether the best idea might not be to have ten crates of beer left on his balcony. And then he actually thought: a dishwasher, well, why not—he'd never buy one, but a dishwasher for free, and it would be quite useful . . . and now this dentist idea. But he didn't need to go to the dentist, and as a rule he wasn't afraid of going to the dentist either. He did fear certain other dates. He'd rather have his wisdom teeth extracted than keep some of those, for instance . . .

Thinking of the list of clients she still had to visit, the fairy was relieved to see Max stop frowning. Soon he raised his head and asked, with a small, almost challenging light in his eyes, "Suppose I wish for an idiot to stop being too idiotic to see his own idiocy?"

Once again the fairy looked surprised, but quite pleasantly surprised this time. She had been fairly sure that a man like Max would end up choosing the most expensive material thing available, as usual. There were clients who asked straight out, "What's the most expensive?" It was the dishwasher.

"That shouldn't really be any problem. Could you explain in a bit more detail?"

"I'm going to have to talk to my business partner any moment now—well, he's my boss, but he's my friend too—anyway, I have to tell him what's wrong with the firm because of him, and he simply refuses to understand. Or else he can't understand."

The fairy nodded. "But bear in mind that you won't remember my visit. So you have to be fairly sure you'll be discussing these problems with your business partner anyway."

"I'll forget all this?"

"Why do you think you've never heard of us before?" The fairy gave Max a moment to adjust to this new idea, and then asked, "Do you still want that wish?"

Briefly, Max was overcome by a feeling that he had free choice of the prizes in a grab bag, and by accident he'd picked something out of the corner of the bag that was full of cheap ballpoint pens and plastic screwdrivers. But then he realized that his wish was not because he wanted to tell Ronnie his opinion straight for once, but because it was up to Ronnie whether Good Reasons did a U-turn or finally collapsed—along with the stock and everyone's jobs. Max wasn't bothered about that; even if he forgot the fairy's visit, he could back out at the last minute. For the sake of his own future, he had no choice but to try making Ronnie see reason. And then Max was flooded by what was almost a hot surge of pleasure as he looked forward to hearing Ronnie beg forgiveness for all the mean things he'd done these last few years, showering him, Max, with gratitude for the words that had opened his eyes.

Max took a deep breath. Then he smiled and said, solemnly, "I still want it."

"Then your wish is granted."

Max still had his arm raised aloft as the waiter put a glass of beer down in front of him.

"Anything else?" he asked, as Max, still looking straight ahead as if dazed, kept his arm in the air.

". . . What?"

"Anything else you wish for?"

Max looked at the full glass, then at the waiter's face, let his arm fall and slowly shook his head. "No, thanks."

When the waiter had gone Max looked at the time. He had to be at the Maria in half an hour. Perhaps he'd better have a coffee first. It seemed he'd almost fallen asleep at the table just now. He was familiar with the feeling: a kind of panic exhaustion often came over him before important meetings.

It happened for the first time during their starter course, and to Max it was like a fairy tale. By way of introducing the subject he'd raised the matter of Nina and her vacation, mentioning the effect of Ronnie's overbearing manner on the office atmosphere, which was nothing brilliant anyway. After Ronnie had listened to him surprisingly quietly, picking at his salad with less and less appetite, he finally put his fork down, took a sip of white wine, lit a cigarette, propped his chin on his hand, and sat there brooding. When the cigarette was half consumed in smoke and ashes, Ronnie raised his head from his hand, brushed the ash off his trousers, still lost in thought, and turned a remorseful, almost sad face on Max.

"Yup, I make myself sick."

A cocktail tomato almost fell out of Max's mouth. "What?"

"Like I said." Ronnie shook his head and stubbed out the cigarette in the ashtray. "Sick to the stomach. I can't think what came over me. Maybe I was jealous of her new boyfriend. I've fancied her myself for quite some time—but now this: oh, hell! Canceling her vacation . . ." Ronnie tapped his forehead. "And Nina's one of the best. What do you think, should I just apologize? No, I tell you what, we'll give her two extra weeks paid for by the firm. She can pick anything she likes, the Caribbean or climbing Mount Everest if she wants—she loves to climb. Or do you think that's a bit too pretentious?"

Ronnie's question and his inquiring gaze left Max completely stunned for a moment. He was about to pick up his knife and fork, but realized that he couldn't swallow another morsel. Instead he took his napkin, wiped his clean mouth, sought support in his wine glass, drank a large gulp and then another, and finally asked, "Are you serious?"

"Good heavens, Max, of course I'm serious. I've behaved like a bastard and I want to put things right. But I'll need your help."

He'd need—what? His *help*? Max didn't think he'd heard Ronnie utter that word these last six years. Of course Ronnie did sometimes need his help, but the way it usually went was along the lines of: Hey, Max, call that wanker from the washing-powder firm and tell him I had him mixed up with someone else—or no, here's a better idea, tell him someone in my family just died and that's why I was in, well, let's say in such a bad mood today—I mean I'm so upset, and I'm sorry I can't call him back myself because I have to order a coffin or something—you'll know what to say, and for heaven's sake buy yourself some decent aftershave for a change, is this place a gay club or what?

Max drank some more wine to be on the safe side, and refilled his glass with a shaking hand before he replied, "I don't know that Good Reasons can afford to pay for trips up Mount Everest right now. But even if it just about could, your generous gesture wouldn't exactly reflect the state of the firm."

"Hm," murmured Ronnie with an attentive expression of concentration such as Max had never seen on his face before, except when Ronnie was talking to someone who might be assumed to be an even bigger bastard than himself.

"Because in case you haven't realized yet," continued Max, feeling the effects of the wine as he gained in confidence, "Good Reasons is on the point of going bust. And since we're on the subject . . ." Max draped one arm over the back of his chair, surprised by the sudden casual assurance of his own posture . . . "since we're on the subject, something like that little episode with Barnes this morning won't save us. Far from it: another couple of misleading press releases and even our most faithful, satisfied clients will wonder if they want to go on working with a double-dealing firm like ours."

And then it happened for the second time: Ronnie saw what an idiot he had been. Max would have loved to look around the restaurant for familiar faces, just to see if there were any witnesses to all this. For it was barely credible: no arrogant justifications or lectures on the necessity of tricking your way through the stock exchange business, not even a bit of defiance or a small evasion along the lines of: you must be joking, Barnes is useless anyway, he ought to have been glad Good Reasons was offering him a chance. No, Ronnie was apologizing, he looked unhappy, he kept on shaking his head.

"It was just so unprofessional! I really must've been one cup short of the full teaset. And if Barnes's agent gets an inkling I was behind it she'll never keep her filthy mouth shut. Everyone in the trade will know about it tomorrow. She's a lezzie, the first time we sat next to each other at a dinner and reception I wrote my hotel room number on her napkin—was there ever trouble!"

Then they decided against ordering anything more to eat, they had another bottle of wine instead, they discussed the present situation of Good Reasons and why things had reached this point. They remembered the way they began. By the time they were on their third bottle they were regretting going public on the stock exchange, and finally they made plans for managing the agency better in the future. The main thing, Ronnie agreed, was to have satisfied staff who enjoyed their work and identified with Good Reasons, so they'd feel committed over and above the minimum and would think up good ideas. In short, they all had to work together as a team again.

"And the hell with the stock ratings!" added Ronnie in such a loud voice that the last two other guests still in the restaurant turned to look at him. "We'll work in our own way again. And if we do it well then the rest will come naturally. Cheers!"

They drank to each other with schnapps, and when they had tipped the liquor down their throats Ronnie leaned over the table and put his arm around Max. "You've no idea what a help you've been to me this evening!"

Max looked over Ronnie's shoulder at the almost empty restaurant, and wondered if this was all a beautiful dream. Almost everything he had so often imagined and wished about Ronnie and their relationship over these last few years had come true today. If their suits hadn't been so expensive and the restaurant so trendy, you might have thought they'd gone back to where they were eight years ago: tall, eloquent Ronnie with his Berlin-New York-Paris business cards, and thoughtful little Max who had lent him the money to print the cards, and had to explain that it sounded silly to speak German with a French accent when you were in Paris. If two such different characters get on with each other at all, their friends had said in those days, then they get on very well. And they did. Both knew their own good qualities and accepted each other's weaknesses, and if they had any differences of opinion, they were still enough like strangers to listen to each other and look for a compromise. But then success came along, the apartments, the cars, and Ronnie began to take his business cards seriously, while Max went on scribbling his address on beermats if anyone wanted it. And so things went on—until this evening.

When they left the Maria around one in the morning, they were swaying drunkenly, and Max took Ronnie's arm. At the taxi stand they were still talking about the good times to begin the next day, and then Ronnie dropped onto the back seat of the cab and Max waved after it. Finally he sat down on the step of a store entrance, lit a cigarette and watched the headlights of the cars gliding up and down the Kudamm. A great city, a great evening.

At some point Max decided he was far too churned up inside to go home yet. He wanted another drink somewhere. The Guevara Club, for instance. Several of the Good Reasons staff patronized the place, so until now he had tended to avoid it. For although he got on well with almost everyone in the office, and he even thought he was quite popular, he could never shake off the feeling that the others toned down their jokes and the agency gossip in front of him. As if Granny had joined their table, so they'd better go easy on the story about group sex with the Pope and try "Heard the one about the two East Frisians?" instead. Now, however, everything was going to be different. The eternal juggling act—showing loyalty to Ronnie while at the same time being a normal member of the staff—was finally over. From tomorrow they'd all be a single team again.

It was just after two when Max entered the bar, which was full of sofas and armchairs and illuminated by muted yellow lighting. Two couples were snuggling into the sofas, the background music was soft jazz on a xylophone, and behind the counter stood a barmaid, smoking. She gave Max a bored nod. He was about to turn away, disappointed, when he decided that at least he'd have a beer as a nightcap. He sat down at the bar, ordered his beer, propped his head on his hands, and watched the barmaid draw it. Tomorrow, then. Ronnie was planning to announce the agency's new spirit at the weekly conference, and in the evening, as Max pictured it, they'd all celebrate together here at the Guevara Club. And he himself would be the undisputed . . .

"Hi, Max."

Max turned his head, and for a moment froze as if he'd heard a shot. Beside him stood Sophie. She took off her jacket, flung it over the back of a chair, sat down on the nearest bar stool, and signaled to the barmaid. Only then did she look at him. As usual, her expression appeared to Max inscrutable.

"What a surprise! I've never seen you here before."

"Hi, Sophie. Well, er . . ." Max forced a smile. "Oh, I've been here a couple of times."

"Ah."

Ah? Ah what? Were you some kind of leper in the agency if you'd paid fewer than a certain number of visits to the Guevara Club? Max felt anger rise in him, until he remembered just in time that everything was different now. Sophie couldn't needle him any more. From tomorrow, because of him and for no other reason, Good Reasons was going to be a completely different firm. And then he'd see who people wanted to go for a drink with.

"But that's all going to change now," he couldn't help saying, hoping as he spoke that Sophie wouldn't demand further explanations. Ronnie hadn't yet announced the new spirit of the agency, and Max was not quite so rolling drunk as to rely one hundred percent on what Ronnie said.

"Why? Going to do some spying on us?"

Sophie had leaned slightly his way, and despite his own alcohol level and the smoky atmosphere Max could smell the drink on her breath.

"Spying?"

"Finding out what the agency staff have to say after work."

Before Max could get out an answer, the barmaid put a beer and a gin and tonic down on the bar in front of them and said, "Enjoy." Sophie picked up her glass, nodded at Max, and took a large gulp.

"You must be crazy," he said finally, as she put her glass down on the bar again.

Ignoring this remark, Sophie asked, "Guess who I was with this evening? Nina. And do you know what we decided?" She leaned slightly his way again, contempt in her glazed eyes.

"No," said Max, instinctively assuming a patronizing smile, "but I'm sure you're about to tell me."

"Very funny. But that's little Max all over: always joking, always trying to spread a little happiness around the office."

"Anything wrong with that?" asked Max with the utmost friendliness, liking himself a great deal in the superior, ironic mood that had suddenly come over him. One of the world's movers and shakers, that was him, taking Sophie's malicious little pinpricks with paternal composure. Maybe she was a lesbian? He'd never thought of that before.

Sophie waved his question away impatiently. "Well, anyway we decided that even without you Ronnie would always be a bastard, but at least he'd be a vulnerable bastard. Because with a slime-bag like you around all the time, smoothing over his faults and fixing things so we just have to grind our teeth and put up with it, we can never have a real row."

Max was frowning, his head tipped to one side. What was she going on about? She seemed totally confused. And she was spraying saliva slightly as she spoke.

"But we *could* have a real row with Ronnie. He's anything you like to call him, but not a coward. He sometimes even has a sense of humor. But with you protecting him! Of course he's glad to have someone keeping trouble off his back—even with the help of that person's own wallet if need be. How much were you planning to pay Nina to take her vacation some other time and keep her mouth shut like a good girl?"

This struck Max as so absurd after his evening with Ronnie that he almost laughed out loud. Automatically, he reached for his coat.

"Just so as to make yourself indispensable! Because I suppose you know that if there's any totally unproductive, unnecessary job at Good Reasons it's yours. And if Ronnie ever realizes that you're standing in the way not just of any unpleasant argument but any constructive one too, he may begin wondering what exactly you can do besides keeping a lid on everything."

Max shook his head and made an effort to sound amused. "This is nonsense. Only just now I convinced Ronnie we must all work together as a team again."

"Sure. With doves of peace perched on our heads for preference. That'd suit you fine: from now on Good Reasons isn't a company listed on the stock exchange and employing a hundred people, it's a happy band of friends with common aims. I can just hear you: relaxed working atmosphere, one big family, net result team spirit and identification with the agency, responsibility resting on everyone's shoulders, creativity, and thus of course enormous success." Sophie took a deep breath, and then hurled her next remarks into Max's face complete with a spray of saliva drops. "Well, there'd really be something to keep the lid on then! And something to smooth over! And fix nicely! Right now the outfit has to go on running somehow, but if we're all supposed to love each other too! . . ."

Max slipped his coat on. This was past bearing!

"Your lousy, anxious attempts at conciliation and understanding—they're the worst thing of all for the agency!"

Without even looking at Sophie again, Max got off his bar stool, put the first banknote he could find in his trouser pocket down on the counter and left the bar.

As he stood in the street looking for a taxi, he wondered what her idea had really been. She probably just wanted to bellyache at him. Bellyache at someone, anyone. How idiotic could you get?

DEFEATED

At twenty-five Paul's prospects were rosy. After two years at the Berlin Film Academy and three highly praised short films, he was considered the outstanding talent of his year by his teachers and the scouts from movie companies and promotional outfits. Even those who disliked his ambition and his unswerving, often fanatical will to get his own way, anywhere and everywhere, had to admit that, compared with his fellow students, he was the only one with the makings of an outstanding career ahead of him. While the others were writing screenplays about the mating game and its problems, comic misunderstandings, or the fate of small-time gangsters, constantly citing Truffaut, Billy Wilder, and (repeatedly) Scorsese's *Mean Streets* as their models, and while they would spend forever in a seminar wondering whether a desperate man who must tell his wife that he's been fired should cross the street stooping slightly or, on the contrary, striding out in an exaggerated manner, all Paul's screenplays dealt with no less than the great themes of love, friendship, and death, his models were Leone, Coppola and Cimino, and he had the desperate man crawling about his apartment on all fours, drunk, throwing up over the passage and his wife, and announcing from time to time that he had been voted top employee of the year in his company. And while the others didn't care one way or the other about this little scene, and would happily have left it out of the filming in the second part of the seminar, Paul extended it. (He had the man take his wife out in the evening to celebrate, and by way of an apology for throwing up on her dress, he took her to an expensive restaurant, where they met the head of personnel who had fired him that morning, and he stabbed his wife before she could learn the truth.) Paul then borrowed the money he needed and made the scene into a six-minute movie in Cinemascope.

With Paul, everything had to be stunning, on the grand scale, and most of the time he was forceful, audacious, and intrepid enough to bring it off. So it hit him all the harder when his forcefulness, audacity, and intrepidity let him down for the first time ever.

While he was working on the screenplay for the film he was making for his finals, a film for which many people were waiting eagerly—it was the story of three unemployed Berliners who hitchhiked to Siberia to prospect for gold, and on the way alternately fell in love, quarreled, parted, were reunited, and finally, with one exception, froze to death—while he was at work on this screenplay something stole into his life. Exactly what and why was a mystery to him for quite some time, not least because he never really asked what it was or why it had come along. Subconsciously, he probably hoped that if he persisted in ignoring this thing that had stolen into his life it would just steal away again.

It began with moments of panic. He briefly felt he was losing his grip, as if he had missed seeing a step and was dropping into the void. It could happen in broad daylight, and whether he was walking, standing, even sitting. If he was sitting it felt like falling for a moment, chair or bench and all. Immediately after that, something like an electric shock went through him and his heart began racing. When it slowed down again the sense of shock and a kind of waking trance remained with him.

He had once been in the Film Academy canteen, on his way to the counter to get a mineral water, during one of these moments. He stood as if paralyzed, almost unnoticed by the others in the canteen, until an acquaintance passed him and inquired, "Another brilliant idea, right?" Paul looked frightened at first, forced a smile, and then, just for something to do and because he didn't trust his legs to take him the rest of the way to the counter, began scratching the back of his neck vigorously. "Yes, right, another brilliant idea. I was just thinking that—." "Keep it for later. I'm ravenous." Paul was still scratching his neck by the time his acquaintance was halfway through a plate of lasagna. When he finally reached the counter he ordered beer.

After that, he had to have beer ready at hand all the time. At first one bottle was enough to allow him to carry on, then he needed two, then four. The moments came more often and lasted longer. Paul began drinking as a precaution, at first only before important meetings, then before any situation that would throw him together with other people, until after four months he was drinking a crate of twenty bottles of beer a day. The border between the exceptional and normality blurred. Paul's life became a sequence of states of mind, always the same, which left him hardly any time for anything else. First was his anxiety before the moment came, then the moment itself, then relief at having survived the moment, and finally anxiety before the approach of the next moment. The one refuge to which he could occasionally resort was work on his screenplay. If it was going well, if he managed to concentrate and immerse himself entirely in its characters and situations, he forgot his anxiety for a while. But usually he found himself just facing clumsy sentences on paper. He often thought of the possible connections. Sometimes he felt his anxiety states were the prerequisite of true creativity, then again he blamed them solely on his fear that the screenplay would fail. For a while his attitude toward writing was like a drug addiction. The more he hoped that it would rescue, distract, and calm him, the more often he sat down at his desk, the weaker the effect. Longer and longer periods at the computer and higher and higher paper consumption soon led to dependency without any relieving effect. After two days and two nights of uninterrupted writing, printing out, deleting, crumpling up paper, and chain-smoking, he finally decided to go cold turkey. His desk would be taboo for a week. Instead, he'd take daily walks, eat regular meals, and watch TV purely for relaxation, not in search of anything of intellectual or cinematic relevance. And the "moments" did subside. He took fewer steps into the void, his heart hardly raced at all. But instead of relaxing and forgetting his work for a while, he thought about it all the more over the next few days. And because he kept strictly to his resolve, avoided the desk, and didn't type a single idea on his laptop, his head soon felt as if it were on the point of exploding. It felt like that the whole time. By the end of the week he was hardly sleeping or eating, he talked to himself out loud in various different tones of voice on his walks, and watching TV he kept thinking how the programs could have been better produced, even during the news. When he finally returned to his desk the first few hours were like a release—until the same old anxiety and desperate search for dialogue set in again the very next day. Still, it seemed far more tolerable than his week of cold turkey.

By now he was seldom going to the Film Academy, and when he did he was more or less drunk, not that anyone noticed. His constant anxiety did not allow him to lose control, stagger about, or babble. It burned up alcohol too fast for the booze to take its normal effect. More and more frequently he asked his girlfriend, Betty, a photojournalist working in Hamburg, not to visit him on her days off. He was at work on his screenplay day and night, he told her, he'd reached a point where it was better to be on his own, or he had the flu, or script conferences, or something. If she came all the same, he made her feel she'd have done better to stay away. He withdrew into his "moments," even when he wasn't having them. He sat in a corner, stared into space, and usually answered questions in the negative. If Betty refused to accept overwork and stress as an explanation, he would switch to the attack. What did she know about his state of mind? After all, what he was trying to create wasn't some photo series about next spring's fashions, it was a new world of his own, a world that would function for an hour and a half. And to create it he needed seclusion, peace and quiet, and now and then a bit of a bender to wash everyday life away. The first few times Betty tried reacting with understanding, then with counterattack: "Before you go creating new worlds you might try making something of this one," and finally with biting observation: "I don't see any new world, I don't even see new words on a piece of paper. All I see is more empty bottles every day." A point came when she stopped visiting him, and a little later they decided not to call each other anymore for the time being.

During these weeks Paul wrote about twenty versions of the third scene. He didn't like any of them. On the second reading, if not before, his sentences, whether dialogue or stage directions, struck him as too ordinary, too lacking in significance, too cursory. By a new world of his own he did not mean something extraterrestrial (which he believed was what Betty had thought he meant—a story about men from Mars or dinosaurs—although in fact Betty had understood him perfectly well). No, he meant a microcosm functioning independently of time and place. For the best movies, Paul thought, were those that made him feel the people on screen didn't need him as a spectator. At some point it occurred to him that because his everyday life and he himself were not important to them, movies like that actually stopped time for an hour and a half and—viewed objectively, since they consisted of film and chemicals—lived forever, so to speak. Suppose you could make such a microcosm yourself? Wouldn't you be stopping time for as much as two or three years, from the first words of your screenplay to the final sound mixing? And since you had made the movie, wouldn't you yourself in a way live forever? From now on these questions wouldn't let him go, they were always haunting the back of his mind, but every time he tried to answer them he felt so exhausted that he soon had to lie down and go to sleep.

About two months after the first "moment," Paul stopped going to the Film Academy entirely, stayed in bed longer and longer after waking up, and almost never left home except to buy cigarettes, beer, and the bare essentials in the way of food. He used the phone solely to negotiate credit in his account with the woman responsible for such things at the bank, or to ask his parents in Gelsenkirchen for "definitely the last" remittance. He picked up the letters and postcards from his anxious friends, who wanted to know where he was, and left them unread, and when there was a knock at the door, or the bell rang, he waited with bated breath until the footsteps went away again. He still spent his afternoons in front of the laptop, but not writing. He just sat there almost motionless for three to four hours, only to lie down in bed again after that in front of the TV set. The one thing that briefly allowed Paul to hope for better times to come was the fact that the intervals between his "moments" were getting longer and longer, until after a week they stopped altogether. Instead, a kind of atrophy came over his senses. He felt as if colors, smells, and sounds were retreating ever further from his perception. Mozart, Bob Dylan, or the garbage truck down in the street—a time came when they all seemed to make the same sound. Similarly, his nose soon found it difficult to decide if the woman next door was simmering beans or frying meatballs. And, most noticeably of all, colors were fading. Even the most garish Saturday evening TV show looked so gray that he spent half the transmission time pressing the brightness and color buttons. And when the sun shone on the chestnut tree in flower down in the backyard, it looked to Paul like a pencil drawing, with its outlines clearer at some times than others. Once he was overcome briefly by panic: Were any of his senses working at all? He hastily felt the wallpaper and the surface of his desk, and just to make sure he slammed a full beer bottle down on his fingers. It hurt, which was a relief. He resigned himself to all the other drawbacks and adjusted to them. Before long he would have been quite confused if anyone poked fun at his bright red built-in kitchen.

Paul was lying in bed watching *Starsky and Hutch*. He hadn't left the apartment for a week, he was living on Honey Smacks, jars of potato salad, butter cookies, and beer, he spent his days almost entirely in front of the television, and when he was walking down the corridor he averted his gaze as he passed the closed study door. He jumped at any noises from next door, at night he went to the front door of the apartment repeatedly to make sure it was locked, and if he dropped anything, or some other small accident happened, he often burst into tears.

After *Starsky and Hutch* Paul switched over to ZDF's early evening series, *Our Teacher Dr. Specht*. Paul let his head sink back on the pillow. *Dr. Specht* was soothing. Paul couldn't watch feature films anymore, let alone good ones. They churned him up and left him unable to sleep. After watching one he had often sat up at his desk half the night, thinking he was making up such snatches of dialogue as "I must be off," "I'll wait for you," "There's always someone waiting," until the next moment it dawned on him with total clarity that he had written them down from memory. *Once Upon a Time in the West* was one of Paul's favorite movies. He had it on video, and in the past, before those "moments" began, if he felt reluctant to sit down and work he often had only to watch two or three scenes from some point in the film to recover his idea of what he was getting at and what was possible. He was obsessed with Leone, who devised stories that almost exactly reflected Paul's own view of the world, and told them in a way that made Paul feel his own concept of narrative was confirmed and understood with every frame and every scene. But when he was brooding over his graduation film and involuntarily remembered

Once upon a Time in the West, an almost crippling horror came over him. If a movie like that could be made, then what was *he* doing?

This evening's episode of *Our Teacher Dr. Specht* was about one schoolboy stealing a hundred marks from another to buy hash. Dr. Specht solved the case, took the hashish away from the guilty boy, who sincerely promised never to do such a thing again, while in his own cheerful way Dr. Specht was also defending himself against the advances of a woman colleague who was in love with him, because in all the excitement over the stolen money he'd forgotten her invitation to coffee and cake, and then in the evening he went to a bar with a rather unkempt friend of his youth, who after a couple of glasses of wine asked him where he could buy some pot in these parts. Cut: Dr. Specht gave the hundred marks back to the boy who had been robbed, and when asked where he had found it replied with a smile, "Minus times minus sometimes makes plus, Sebastian, in life as well as in mathematics." The final credits rolled.

Not good. But not all that bad either. Well, it was an early evening soap. Suppose he made that kind of thing?

Paul took a bottle of beer out of the crate by his bed, opened it, and switched over to the Pro Sieben channel. Some kind of comedy show. Man and woman sitting in a bar on their first date, the man making slips of the tongue like, "It's in the mornings I have a problem getting it up—I mean getting up."

Or something of that nature.

There was tennis on Eurosport. A first-round match on sand between two Spaniards Paul had never heard of. Boring rallies going on for minutes on end, brute force, not a spark of intelligence in the play. Paul finished his beer, opened the next bottle, and thankfully realized that the monotonous way the balls went back and forth was making him feel drowsy. Although he spent almost all day in bed, he never slept for more than two or three hours.

When there was a knock on his front door toward the end of the second set, he didn't hear it at first. Then the knocking grew louder, and for a moment Paul couldn't identify this new sound and bent over the TV set in some annoyance, until he realized what it was and gave a start of surprise. He quickly muted the sound, quietly put the beer bottle down beside his bed, sat up and listened.

"Open the door, Paul! It's me, Sergei!"

The knocking became a hammering.

"Don't be a bloody fool! I heard you had the TV on! And I'm not going away until you talk to me!"

Paul looked around the room with a hunted expression. All tidy, all normal. Except perhaps for the crate of beer beside the bed . . .

"Paul!"

On tiptoe, Paul took the crate into the kitchen. He inspected the kitchen as well, and it too was tidy. Perhaps excessively tidy. He took a couple of newspapers off the neat stack in the corner, threw them down at random, and spread them over the kitchen table. Then he turned on the radio, looking for a station playing cheerful music.

"Look, I'm going to kick this door in if I have to! Or call the firefighters!"

He found something Cuban, conga music and guitars. At the same time he looked at the kitchen clock. An old thing bought in the flea market. He hadn't wound it for weeks. Where was his watch? Still on tiptoe, he hurried into the study.

"Right, I've had enough of this!"

Feet began thudding against the door; the whole building was probably listening. Paul glanced at his watch, ran back, wound up the kitchen clock and moved the hands to eight-thirty. Then he stopped for a moment and tried to concentrate. He walked to the door slowly, making a lot of noise.

"Okay, okay! Just coming."

The kicking stopped. When Paul opened the door his friend was leaning against the wall, hands in his jacket pockets, scrutinizing him with cool curiosity. If he was relieved he didn't show it.

Paul beamed at him. "Hi, Sergei! What's the assault and battery for? Or is it how they usually knock at doors in Serbia?"

Sergei had been in Belgrade for the last three months, making a documentary. He did not react at all to Paul's joke. Slowly, he pushed himself away from the wall and took a step toward the door.

"May I?"

Paul tried to keep on beaming in the way he thought appropriate for a reunion with his best friend after three months, but it was getting harder and harder to beam under Sergei's unremittingly cool gaze.

"Sure, come in. Why ask in that funny way?"

Should he hug Sergei? They always did when they hadn't seen each other for over a week. But now . . . somehow it didn't seem right.

Sergei came into the apartment, and Paul closed the door.

"I asked the way you'd ask someone you haven't heard from for two months, someone who doesn't pick up the phone, doesn't answer letters, and tells his girlfriend he's joined the ranks of men of genius."

Sergei said this as if he did not expect an answer. Hands still deep in his jacket pockets, he looked up at the ceiling. "Could we have the light on?"

"Er, no. Sorry, the bulb went. But we're not going to stand around in the hall, are we?"

Paul sounded amused, although he was in fact annoyed, for the bulb had gone out only two days ago. Now Sergei probably thought he'd been living without a light in the hall for weeks. Ought he to explain? Was it more normal to live without a light in the hall, or to make it your priority to tell your friend, after three months apart, that up to two days ago you *were* living with a light in the hall? Why did Sergei ask anyway? He'd never have noticed a thing like that before.

Was he trying to corner him somehow? Because he'd been out of touch for a while? All very well for Sergei: he made documentaries, he didn't have to invent a storyline, write dialogue, think about the cast—he just had to choose a subject, point the camera at it, and leave the rest to the cutting-room table. Of course, Paul knew it wasn't quite that simple, but all the same . . .

"Considering that we're not going to stand around in the hall, we've been here quite some time already," said Sergei.

Paul looked back at him. Why the ironic tone of voice? He'd only turned briefly to the coat rack, as if looking for a hanger for Sergei's jacket.

"Well, do we go anywhere else now?"

"Sure, into the kitchen. I was only looking to see if there was a hanger for your jacket."

"A hanger for my jacket?" Sergei looked down at his hooded sports jacket. "Oh, I think I can manage without."

The kitchen radio was now broadcasting a feature about a South American death cult. When Paul made haste to switch over to another station he almost knocked the radio off the fridge.

"The things those radio people think up!" He smiled at Sergei, shaking his head. "Just now they were playing hot music, you go out for a minute and you come back to find them broadcasting this."

"Mhm." Sergei sat down at the kitchen table and glanced at the newspaper lying open on it in front of him.

After Paul had tuned to a jazz station he leaned back against the kitchen cupboard and folded his arms. But it immediately struck him that folded arms look defensive, so he let them drop to his sides, was momentarily at a loss for somewhere to put his hands, and finally dug them half-way into his trouser pockets. Not all the way, so as not to give the impression that he was trying to strike a robust attitude.

"I was reading, must have dozed off, that's why I didn't hear you knock at first."

Sergei looked up from the paper and inspected him expressionlessly. "Looking for a job?"

"What?"

Sergei tapped the newspaper. "Positions Vacant: sales managers, personnel managers, bookkeepers. Your new line of work?"

"Oh, that . . ." Paul's mouth remained open as he took a quick glance at the kitchen table. Was this some trick? No, the paper really was open at the jobs section. How stupid! "That's for research purposes. My movie's about the unemployed. A bit later I'll have to go to the job center and meet people there, of course, but for now . . ."

"How's the screenplay going, then?"

"Well, so-so, sometimes good, sometimes not so good. But I just happened to have a moment today when I thought, ah, now I have it: the core of the whole thing, the metaphor hovering over it all—understand?"

"And the metaphor would be what?"

Paul tightened his lips and looked at the floor as he sought for words. He had often reacted to Betty's questions in the same way: like a physicist asked to explain the theory of relativity in simple sentences that a layman could understand.

"Well, I can't explain straight off like that. It's still more of a vague idea than anything else. I know where I want to go now, but I'm not there yet—understand?"

"Don't say 'Understand?' when you're not telling me anything."

"But I was only saying I—"

"Where's the screenplay?"

Paul stopped short, feeling hot under the collar. "In my study."

"Can I take a look?"

Until three months ago it had been rare for either of them to finish writing something without the other reading it several times and saying what he thought. They even used to show each other the love letters they wrote. Back then, Sergei's question would almost have been an insult.

Paul grasped the nettle. For the first time since opening the door to Sergei he looked him in the eye and smiled apologetically, as if he had to cancel a party invitation.

"Not yet. It's silly, maybe, but I feel kind of superstitious about this one. I don't want to let anyone see it until it's finished. The whole story comes to a head in the very last scene, and only if that scene works will the rest work too. Underst—I mean, that's clear, isn't it?"

"There isn't any screenplay."

"What?"

"Betty said there isn't any screenplay. Any amount of empty beer bottles, pages of crossed-out dialogue from Leone movies, but nothing you could call a screenplay, or even the beginning of a screenplay."

"That's nonsense!" Paul took his hands out of his trouser pockets and moved away from the fridge. "I mean, what does Betty know about it?" He walked around the table and began folding up the newspapers with an air of resolution. "And since when did you take so much notice of what she says?"

"Let me see it."

"I . . ." Paul straightened up. He was holding the papers to his chest, his fingers clutching them tight. What was Sergei's idea? Bursting in here, carrying on like God Almighty! Had he asked Sergei for anything? "I don't want to."

"Okay," said Sergei, "then I'll look for it myself." He was about to rise to his feet, but Paul stepped forward to bar his way.

"Don't do that!"

"Look here . . ." Sergei looked into Paul's wide, panic-stricken eyes and wondered what the hell this fuss was all about. "Have you lost your marbles or what?"

"I said I don't want to show you!"

"There's a lot of other things you could do right now, though: open your door, for instance, or let people know you're still alive. So I don't care what you don't want to do."

For a moment Paul held Sergei's challenging gaze, then looked aside, sensed the tension draining away from his body, and the next moment felt nothing but weakness. Slowly and heavily he leaned one hand on the table, put the newspapers down, drew up a chair and sat on it. Now and then he cast Sergei a timid glance, as if pleading for understanding, without knowing what he really wanted to be understood. Finally he said, "I can't do it."

"Can't do what?"

"Anything. I'm scared. Of the screenplay, of failure, of life, of death . . ." And then Paul described the way he'd gone downhill these last three months. Sergei listened, nodded, opened beer bottles.

Around twelve they drank the last two bottles of beer from the crate, and when they had sat in silence for a while Sergei said, "Well, we can fix that." Paul smiled, exhausted.

Later, when Paul was staring at the ceiling in the light of the bedside lamp, hearing Sergei's snores from the room next door, and for the first time seriously thinking of dashing everyone's expectations, chucking in his graduation movie, and swallowing his greatest defeat to date, the fairy came to see him.

She hovered at the end of his bed and said, "Good evening."

Paul sat up with a start and raised his hands defensively. Even the fairy aura didn't affect the ease with which he presently took fright.

"Don't be scared," said the fairy. "I am a fairy and I've come to grant you a wish. I apologize for the late hour, but I had so much to do today. I was really going to come tomorrow, but I was told that your case was particularly urgent." The fairy gave him a friendly smile. As she did so she glanced briefly around the room, noticing the empty beer bottles, an open carton of Honey Smacks, and the smell of bedclothes that hadn't been changed for a long time. Spotlessly clean and tidy as the apartment was, the bedlinen, Paul's clothes, and the fridge stank because he hardly noticed smells any more.

Paul slowly lowered his hands and stared at her in horror. It didn't bother him much that she said she was a fairy, or that he could see the TV set right through her. Over the last few weeks Paul had fought his way through so many nightmares, delusions, and imaginary doomsday scenarios that one more fantastic apparition wasn't going to throw him. Far from it; the fairy seemed naturally associated with a whole set of beings (such as God, the Devil, and the black cat next door) with whom he had regularly held conversations recently. It was probably rare for anyone to accept a fairy's reality more easily than Paul did just now. But for that very reason his horror intensified by the second and became a genuine state of shock. Because as he saw it, there could be only one logical reason for the fairy's appearance.

In a stifled voice, he asked, "Am I dying?"

"Dying?" The fairy looked surprised. "Goodness, no. What makes you think that?"

"I thought . . ." Paul stopped. Then it seemed as if all his weight was draining away, and he felt so light that he had to cling to the edge of the mattress. "Because . . . well, it was just that . . . are you sure?"

"Of course I'm sure. We almost never visit dying people. Their wishes are nearly always the same, and we can't grant them."

Paul had no idea what the fairy was talking about, nor was he interested. He could have shouted for joy.

"Right, so now calm down again and try to remember your wish."

"What wish?"

"The wish you expressed or thought some time in the last few days. If you hadn't made one I wouldn't be here."

"*One* wish?" For the first time in weeks Paul laughed with relief, and when he heard himself he laughed even more.

The fairy waited until his fit of mirth was over. "For all I know you made twenty wishes, but I can only grant one. The following areas are out, though: immortality, health, money, love."

When the fairy had finished her patter, Paul lay there for a while without moving, looking at her with increased attention. "Why immortality?"

"You can't ask me that. I didn't make the rules."

"And suppose, let's say . . ." Paul ran his tongue over his lips. If he didn't have to die, or at least if he had more time—why would he mind if this screenplay was a failure? He'd just try again and again. And perhaps the movie wouldn't have to be quite so significant and eternal if he was a little bit more eternal himself. "How about just living an extra two hundred years?"

The fairy shook her head. "Almost every extended lifespan comes under the heading of immortality. I mean, in exceptional cases people can have a few days or even a whole week, but there have to be good, clearly defined reasons."

"Good reasons?"

"Well, suppose you wish—it's not very likely at your age, but just as an example—suppose you wish someone to get a certain message after your death. Because you're afraid you won't be brave enough to give it while you're alive. Then we could arrange something. Or suppose you wanted to finish your life spending a weekend with your wife in Venice or somewhere. We could just add that on. Do you understand?"

"Yes, but . . . " Paul felt himself gaining strength. The fairy wanted a good reason, and he had one. He leaned forward. "Look, I'm a movie director and a writer, and I have some really great films in my head. I mean movies that only I can make. Even if I told someone else the storylines, no one could make the movies the way I imagine them. They'd feel shoddy, they wouldn't ring true, because no one else would put my basic idea, my own melody, my purpose into them. That's why I need more time . . ." Paul's head was thrust eagerly toward the fairy as he bent his urgent, feverish, imploring glance on her. "Or I'll never do it!"

"Too bad," said the fairy "Then you won't do it." She was feeling slightly annoyed with the boss for rushing her like that. Those in fear of death did count as urgent cases, but everyone knew that in the long run artists never really got into their stride without the fear of death. They needed it. So she could perfectly well have come tomorrow, even next week.

"But you can't make up your mind so quickly! You just said, if there's a good reason. And my movies . . ."

"Your movies," the fairy interrupted, "have nothing whatever to do with it. I've told you the rules, and you can't change them. The only alternative to a wish that's within the rules is no wish at all. Apart from which, it strikes me that for someone who thought just now he was going to die, for whatever reasons, wishing to live forever is rather excessive."

Paul gave the fairy a furious glance. Why didn't his movies have anything to do with it? Was she visiting *him* and asking to know *his* wish, or did she just go flying off to anyone to grant any kind of wish? So long as it kept the rules. And why was it excessive to wish to live forever, when he had so much important work to do?

"Young man, I really must ask you to get around to your wish. You're keeping other people waiting, people who'd be delighted to have wishes within the bounds of possibility granted."

"Other people!" Paul made a dismissive gesture. "What kind of wishes do they have? A new car, three weeks in Ibiza?"

"Calm down! And in case you didn't understand me, you don't have unlimited time for making your wish."

"Oh no? Then in that case. . . !" Paul felt like simply sending the fairy away.

"Try to remember your wishes over the last few days. Living two hundred years extra isn't likely to have been among them."

"You have no idea!"

"Yes, I do. People don't wish for anything so fantastic. You only thought of it when I told you what's not possible."

"Then why mention it at all?"

"I'm sorry. Usually it makes my visits go more easily. But in your case . . . yes, you're probably right, I ought to have kept my mouth shut, but that doesn't get us any further now."

The fairy's conciliatory tone defused Paul's anger. It did take him a little while to wave good-bye—as he saw it—to the gates of Paradise and return to ordinary life, but finally he said, sighing, "Very well: what I've wished for most of all recently is not to feel afraid."

"There, you see? Now, could you put it a little more precisely? Do you mean you don't want to feel afraid at all, even if your house is burning down or war breaks out? Or is it a matter of some special fear?"

"I'm afraid of failing. With my screenplay, my movie, my work. I've done nothing at all for weeks for fear of doing something wrong."

"Well then . . ." The fairy hesitated. Now she'd been putting pressure on the young man, and was it his fault if the boss had sent her out so late, although it meant working overtime? "Are you sure you won't miss feeling just a little afraid now and then?"

"Miss feeling afraid? Not likely!"

"Just as you like," said the fairy. "And your wish is granted."

Next morning Sergei persuaded Paul to go to a café for breakfast, and for the first time in weeks he mingled with other human beings again. As if everything was perfectly normal, Sergei told him about Belgrade, they talked about people they knew, complained of their colleagues, and Paul was glad that Sergei didn't mention yesterday evening. Only as they parted, because Sergei had an appointment to keep, did he ask, "Shall I come back this evening?"

In fact for the first time in ages Paul, reassured by Sergei's presence, had enjoyed more than three hours' unbroken sleep last night. All the same, he said, "Thanks, but let's phone each other later. I feel so much better after our talk yesterday, I can start thinking straight about everything at last. And I may be better off on my own doing that."

"Okay, if you promise me not to lie in bed watching lousy soaps."

"I promise," said Paul, and was surprised to find how sure he felt of keeping his word. This morning nothing drew him back to the quagmire of the last few weeks, compounded of *Starsky and Hutch*, Honey Smacks, and beer. Far from it: he was looking forward to buying some proper food, opening the windows of his apartment wide, listening to music, and exchanging a few words with the neighbors on the stairs.

At midday—with potatoes and asparagus simmering on the stove, the sound of a Mozart violin concerto coming from the study, and some kids crowing out loud as they played football in the backyard—Paul decided to put his screenplay aside for a while, until he felt far enough away from it to begin again with a clear head. But during that evening and the following day he caught himself wondering with increasing frequency what the story really had to do with him. Was *he* unemployed? And if he were, would he hitchhike to Siberia? Did people go prospecting for gold these days? And if so, did he know any of them? Basically, he had no idea about any of this. Who did he think he was kidding?

He and Sergei spoke on the phone every evening about this and that, ordinary everyday things. Sergei asked how Paul was, and Paul said truthfully he was feeling better every day. At the end of the week he returned to the Academy for the first time, and then went to a bar with a few students. He noticed a man at the next table sitting over a single beer all evening, looking around every time someone came through the door. While his acquaintances talked about movies that had just opened, Paul couldn't shake off the image of the man at the next table. Making one beer last almost two hours meant he was either broke or wanted to keep a clear head. Because he was waiting for someone, and they had something important to discuss? Waiting for his wife? His lover? Was he having an affair? He, Paul, had often waited in assorted bars for Betty when she was still officially living with someone else. He knew all about waiting around with that kind of excited anticipation, happy but anxious too, wondering whether everything would still be the same as last time.

"Good to see you back," one of the students said, parting from Paul as they went out into the street, and the others said, "See you tomorrow," and waved, and then they all disappeared in different directions. Paul decided to walk home, and on the way he went on thinking of those first months with Betty. He'd never been so much in love before, he believed he had found the only woman in the world for him, he thought he'd never so much as look at another girl. Sheer rapture. Okay, so that changed later, but no movie lasts all that long either.

When he told Sergei his idea over the phone that night, Sergei said: "Hmph? A story about waiting around and being in love? What *is* the story?"

"It's the state of mind in itself. I'm not after any particular plot, no startling effects, just the meticulous observation of an exceptional situation."

"An exceptional situation? Being in love with a woman who has another man?"

"Well, they'll get together at the end, of course."

"Of course. Can I give you some advice? Go back to your prospectors in a couple of weeks' time. That one *is* a story, and a good one, so stop giving me all this Eric Rohmer-style tripe."

"I don't call it tripe—at least, not the way I imagine it. The whole thing is set in Berlin, of course, and we have the great city's special rhythm, its bars and dives, its billiard saloons, the U-Bahn, the Turkish market, backyards, all in a kind of blue and white light—I can see it all before my eyes already."

"Yes, so can I," sighed Sergei.

"You know, it dawned on me over the last few days that the prospectors' story doesn't really have anything to do with me."

"Even if it doesn't it's still exciting. And while I'm very glad you're feeling better and your fears have gone away— well, you ought at least to be afraid of boring people rigid with a 'state of mind in itself' shot in blue and white light."

"So who cares if I'm going to bore some people? The main thing is I feel good about the story. And it's only a movie. No movie's ever going to change the world, and I have plenty of time to make others. Anyway, right now a quiet little snapshot seems just the right thing for me."

"Oh. Listen, I'm afraid I have to pack my bags now, I'm off to Belgrade again first thing tomorrow. But I'll be back in a week, and then we'll discuss it at our leisure. Don't go messing everything up now."

"Okay. Have fun, and don't get all stressed out in Belgrade."

"Oh, but I will. That's my idea exactly."

When they had hung up, Paul shook his head. For the first time he realized that Sergei must have a problem. The fanatical way he threw himself into his projects, practically killing himself with every film—you really had to call it rather hysterical. Furthermore, a six-hour documentary about the history of Belgrade in the twentieth century— wouldn't anything less do? Was he planning to explain the entire Yugoslavian war, all Europe maybe, or even better, the whole world? A courageous effort, certainly, but didn't his courage perhaps rise from a fear of not being up to the demands of certain people? The demands of the TV editors? His friends? His parents? The public? Himself? And even if the symptoms of that fear were Sergei's perfectionism, his obsessions, and a certain kind of genius—wouldn't they be the ruin of him? And was a film worth that, even if it was a masterpiece? No, he'd have to talk to Sergei about this: what ultimately mattered in the end was whether you'd had a halfway good time. And if the end product was only mediocre—well, was that the end of the world?

Then Paul put on a soothing Ben Webster CD, made a cup of tea, sat on the sofa, and thought at his leisure of the way his movie should begin. Was the man in the bar drinking beer or wine? White wine, perhaps, it could be sparkling, unlike red wine a sparkling white could hint at his agitated state of mind. That might even work in the title. *White Wine, Black Nights*, or *White Wine and Black Bread*—perhaps the woman only ever ate bread? Well, he'd be sure to think up something good, he had no fears on that account.

SELF-DEFENSE

On the afternoon of September 14, 2001, Victor Radek—named after Victor Jara, the Chilean songwriter murdered by the military junta, who had once been revered by his mother—Victor Radek was sitting beside his girlfriend, Natasha, on the sofa of a suite in the Kempinski Hotel watching, for the umpteenth time, TV pictures of the airplanes crashing into the World Trade Center. Next came the U.S. President vowing revenge. After that an interview with Bin Laden in which he announced his plans to save the Islamic world by waging holy war.

"If he carries on saving his world this way, there soon won't be any of it left," said Natasha.

Victor nodded abstractedly. He and his band had a concert tomorrow, and he still didn't know whether they ought to cancel it.

He couldn't really imagine singing *Darling, let's just drink another* tomorrow evening.

They watched Bin Laden in silence for a while, until the telephone rang. Victor rose to his feet and went over to the writing desk.

"Radek."

"Reception here, Herr Radek. A visitor for you."

"Who is it?"

"Your mother. I'll put her on the . . ."

"Wait a moment!"

"Yes, sir?"

Victor hesitated. Then he said, "This must be some kind of bad joke. My mother's dead."

"Er . . . what?"

"You heard."

"I'm really sorry, Herr Radek, how was I to . . ."

"Okay."

Victor put the receiver down. When he turned around, he saw Natasha's frightened face.

The doctor had told her to exercise more. The doctor was an idiot, of course. Who'd kept advising her to have the operation? And now, three months later, she was still walking with a crutch.

The healing process takes time, Frau Radek. Try to approach the situation in a more positive way.

Approach it, when she could hardly move at all! And a man like that had studied at university! But he had a Mercedes outside his door and a villa in the fashionable suburb of Zehlendorf! If she'd given her customers such advice, she wouldn't own so much as a moped today. But it made no difference to doctors. They could advise and diagnose anything they fancied and still go home in a Mercedes in the evening. Not that she didn't have a good car herself. A Volvo. But she'd earned it. Apart from which, of course she didn't care a hoot for the make of a car. Anyway, she hadn't struggled— yes, struggled!—all her life for that kind of thing.

Undecided, Frau Radek stood by the board where the keys hung near the front door of her apartment. Should she take the car now or go on foot? Even if the doctor was an idiot, a little exercise might in fact do her good. And if she walked she'd have the opportunity to think in peace, working out everything she was going to say to Victor. Among other things, in the context of those terrorist attacks in America. There was going to be war. War! What a terrible thought! The whole world was in danger! Including Victor. And herself. That made everything seem relative. What's more, you could never find a place to park in the city.

She left her car key hanging on the board, turned to the coat rack, and put a coat on. She'd walk, then. Of course it would be painful. And people would stare. An old lady hobbling along. Well, let them stare. She'd never minded much what people thought. And they'd always stared anyway. Back in '72, for instance, when she opened Bandiera Rossa in the Charlottenburg district. The sign was only just going up over the shop door when the first neighbor came along. "So what's that mean?"

"Red Flag."

"Ah. A flag on special offer, is it?"

"This is a record store."

"Oh, I thought . . . kind of misleading, innit?"

"Word will soon get around."

"Don't s'pose you got something classical? I like classics, I do."

"We have classics here too."

"But I don't want no Russians. Too sad."

"We don't stock just Russian composers. And you can order anything from us."

"Ah. Well now, with that name, I'd have to think it over. Kind of a symbol, innit? Nothing to do with the records, see what I mean?"

And so it went on for the first few months, day in, day out. Those were the friendly ones, too. The shop window had been smashed four times, stinkbombs had been thrown into the premises seven or eight times, and for years the façade had been repeatedly plastered with graffiti. Then there were the tourist parties from Nuremberg or Passau or other places in West Germany, shaking their heads over the big red star-shaped neon sign and wondering indignantly, at the top of their voices, whether in view of the proximity of the Wall and the daily threat of Russian invasion this wasn't positively criminal. But none of it could get her down. She'd run Bandiera Rossa for twenty-eight years, and the store had been known to left-wingers all over the country. It still was. People often came up to her in the street, people she hardly knew, to say what a shame it was that Bandiera Rossa had closed and the site was occupied by the thousandth Italian deli in town instead. But the proprietor of the building had given her the right to nominate the next tenant, and the Italian, who was not in fact Italian but Syrian, had offered her the largest sum as key money. Was it her fault that there were no young people today with enough courage and sense of ethics to run a politically committed record store?

Or rather, people *used* to come up and speak to her in the street. Hardly anyone did now. It was that crutch, of course: bad luck looks as if it could be catching.

Hobbling, Frau Radek hauled herself down the stairs. She glanced into the letterbox at the entrance of the building. Only junk mail. How quickly you were forgotten. Once she'd made sure she gave only the shop address, to keep her letterbox from overflowing. All the small record companies, the musicians she had helped, some of whom she'd been partly responsible for discovering (there was even a Bandiera Rossa label in the late seventies and early eighties, with disks from songwriters all over the world), and the concert promoters, and the House of Culture—they'd all showered her with invitations and letters expressing their gratitude. But now . . . well, *she* had never acted that way. She never forgot anyone, she took care of everyone right to the last. There was Margarete, for instance, her last employee. Well, of course she couldn't let her take over the store, even if Margarete had wanted it. Such a shy, dreamy creature. You needed dynamic qualities for a store like that—you needed to be able to knuckle down to it, get a move on, do a thorough job. After three months at the most it would all have been too much for Margarete, and it was up to her to save both the store and Margarete herself from that. Was her life's work simply to go bust like some vegetable shop? Moreover, Margarete didn't have a pfennig to pay her for the key money. However, she had devoted whole evenings to Margarete's future, invited her to drink a glass of wine, and helped her to see that if she was ever to get anywhere in life she must leave her boyfriend, who fancied himself a musician but just took drugs and talked big. Frau Radek had even gone so far as to cite her own son's example.

"Take Victor. Listen to his music. His lyrics. I may be his mother, but I have to say that art is a matter of hard work, and that's something Victor has never understood. He has talent, yes, but just talent . . . it's supposed to be punk rock, something like the Tote Hosen band—oh, well. I know all about the beginnings of punk rock, back when the first disks came over from England. Now that was something else! He just doesn't work at it hard enough."

"Work at punk rock . . . ?"

"Punk rock's an art too, and the idle don't create art."

"But Victor—I mean he's successful. He makes a lot of money."

"For now. But wait till fashions change. He'll be left high and dry with his songs: *Darling, let's just drink another* and *Never, never comb your hair*. So that kind of thing's a hit, but all on a private level. Makes no claims, nothing. And does anyone still sing like that when they're forty, on just two chords? Oh, the fans will melt away then. He'll suddenly find out about real life! A gig in Darmstadt or Reutlingen now and then, otherwise he'll be living on social security and going from door to door."

"Well, but . . . I mean, he's doing his own thing, right?"

"Doing his own thing! Try doing your own thing when you're old and no one wants to know about you any more."

"But how can you tell in advance . . . I mean, if you're always thinking about that, then—"

"Then what? Then you're facing reality and preparing for it—simple! But I didn't mean to talk about my son."

"Oh, but you often do."

"Because I'm worried, that's the only reason. He just won't listen. He thinks life will always go on like this: success, money, the hell with what his mother says—"

"I don't know, but . . . but I'd be glad if my boyfriend sometimes said the hell with what his mother says."

"I can't say I've met your boyfriend very often, but my impression so far . . . in any case, you must help him to make more of himself."

"Oh, I don't think I want to do that. I mean, I'm his girlfriend and not . . . well, as I see it, helping people that way somehow doesn't go with love."

"It goes with love in particular. Love above all. Everyone can do with help and good advice. I've been helping people all my life."

When Frau Radek moved away from the letterbox to leave the building, she found a car barring her way. A great big Opel, belonging to her neighbor on the fourth floor. And he was unemployed too. A computer specialist, fired three months ago. But still driving his great big car! It probably mattered more than anything to him. He'd be in for a shock when the war began. Soaring gasoline prices and so on.

"Hello!"

No answer. The car was empty. Was she supposed to squeeze past it? When she could hardly even walk?

"Hello! I can't get by! There's a car in the way!"

A door slammed behind her on the stairs.

"Hello!"

"Yes, yes, just coming!"

Mister Computer Specialist! Unemployed and still acting the businessman in a great hurry. Parking the car right outside the door where no one could miss it. Leather seats, CD player, leather-covered steering wheel—that's men for you!

The computer specialist came downstairs. Lilac suit, blow-dried hair. "Oh, it's you."

Frau Radek gave him a bitter smile. "As you see, I'm not too mobile at the moment." She waved her crutch in the air. "So perhaps you wouldn't mind remembering my disability next time you leave your car outside. Five meters further on would be enough."

"I was in a hurry."

Frau Radek could see that he was silently cursing her. He hated her because she saw through him. An old cow living alone, hardly able to walk, and she of all people saw his total mediocrity. No doubt he could fool those young floozies he sometimes brought home, but she had only to look into his selfish, envious, angry eyes to know he was just a particularly unattractive example of the male of the species. And she knew about *them*, oh, didn't she just! She had never, ever, taken anything lying down from men. Not even Victor's father, whom she had really loved. But ultimately he too was only a man who needed more loving care and praise than a whole kindergarten of children. So she'd had to decide between her work and Victor on the one hand, and a love full of quarrels, jealousy, and alcohol on the other. She'd always told Victor about it, even when he was very small, so that he would understand why they were not what's called a normal family: I left your father for your sake, just for you! That was quite something, wasn't it? And what must Victor do, once he thought he was grown up, but say, "Thanks, but I'd rather not be told quite so often that my parents divorced purely for my sake." Guilt feelings, indeed! His then girlfriend had probably taught him all that psychobabble. That was her all over: twice around the houses, upstairs and downstairs, before she could finally bring herself to say, "Yes, I think I might like another cup of coffee if there's still any in the pot." Luckily she didn't last long, although Victor was so upset about it, unable to concentrate on his final school exams, that she herself even tried to save the relationship. She'd visited the girl at home specially, she'd explained how young men were like that: they had to gain experience, try themselves out, and there was no need for her, the girlfriend, to make such a fuss merely because Victor was sleeping with other girls too, that was just biology. Well, so it came out later that that wasn't the trouble at all, and the girl hadn't known anything about Victor's other adventures before—but it was a fact that she had tried to help them both, even though she didn't particularly like the girl. How could she guess that young people today were so uptight about sex? The girl had practically come to blows with her, and then shouted at her to go away— and only a moment before she'd been thinking: maybe we don't get on so well together, but we're both women, some kind of solidarity must be possible. Because she'd have liked to know a few things about Victor's private life. He was always so unforthcoming to her at the time. But no, not a trace of solidarity. Young things like that girl had only themselves to blame if men treated them badly.

The Opel started, and Frau Radek called triumphantly, "Thank you very much." Then she hobbled down the steps outside the building. She could still look after herself. Even if everyone abandoned her, and even her own son wasn't speaking to her anymore—she wasn't done for yet! She turned right in the direction of the Bayerischer Platz and hobbled vigorously on. Victor had been difficult for a long time. Since his thirteenth year, to be exact. Puberty, of course, and he still wasn't out of it. But before that everything had gone so well. When he came home for the weekend they'd always had a really good time, and once a month she'd driven him back to his boarding school herself to make sure everything was all right. She'd talked to the teachers and his fellow pupils, straightening things out. And were there ever things to be straightened out! For instance, no one in the school knew how sensitive and vulnerable Victor was. Or how talented and intelligent either. She'd had to tell the other boys and girls all about it. Admittedly, Victor hadn't liked that, but her motto was: tell the truth and shame the Devil. Victor was homesick—well, they could talk about all that. But he didn't want to leave the boarding school either, though she'd offered to take him away. Later he once said he was very grateful to her for sending him away to school at the age of nine, which meant it was possible he'd got away from her early enough, and in spite of his homesickness he had some inkling of it at the time. Well, of course you could always make up stories about that kind of thing in retrospect. The fact was, however, that she'd toiled day and night to pay the boarding school fees. Because it wasn't just any boarding school, it was the best and most modern around. Think of all the celebrities who'd gone to the school! People always stared when she mentioned its name and said her son was there. She, the daughter of a postal worker and a cleaning lady, and now with a son at that boarding school—she liked saying so, too, and why not? It was something she could be proud of. And everything had been wonderful until—well, until Victor reached puberty. Suddenly he didn't want her to fetch him from school anymore. Well, he'd reckoned without her! She wasn't going to let him stop her caring about his well-being. So his mother suddenly embarrassed him? She, of all people: the legendary dynamo of the left-wing record store, well known in the music business, on terms of familiarity with many musicians, popular with her customers, committed, open-minded, and more youthful than most young people? It was just a joke for her son to treat her like any ordinary mother. Inside her head, anyway, she was still younger than all the girlfriends he began to have around then. When she remembered the one with the horse posters! Horse posters! She'd really had to do something about that. Her son was not an idiot. Hadn't she put posters of Angela Davis and Che Guevara up on his wall almost before he could walk? So maybe she shouldn't have called the parents of the girl with the horse posters, but how was she to know they'd kick up such a fuss? Imagine saying the boarding school was no better than a brothel! That was dentists for you. Anyway, many of Victor's fellow pupils would have been glad to have a mother like her. But Victor didn't realize that his mother was his best friend, that was the problem. To this day. Yet she was the only one who really worried about him. As for all the people who came flocking around him these days, he couldn't trust them. None of them would tell him the truth. They only saw his success, his money—just like Margarete. (What a good thing she hadn't let Margarete take over the store!) And none of them dared say his lyrics didn't rhyme and their subjects were sometimes positively reactionary, the music ignored every rule of composition, and the band in general carried on with rowdy ostentation.

Frau Radek crossed the Bayerischer Platz. She recognized a concert promoter she'd worked with once or twice in the past, sitting in a car waiting at the lights. No, she felt she didn't really need to wave. He'd even chased after her once—that fat fellow! Well, let him see her now: hobbling along, but with her chin up. Him in his BMW! And he'd never amounted to anything. It was probably his connections with the city council. She'd never have stooped to that. The men's club. Should she just go over and glance in at the car window? "Fallen upstairs, have you, bought a BMW?" A sassy remark in her old style. And then, amused, "Some of us can only afford a Volvo!" He'd know what a Volvo meant.

But then the lights changed, and Frau Radek had to wait on the pedestrian island and watch the concert promoter drive past her.

And Victor listened to such people. His record company, for instance. It was large, successful, famous—yes, it was all that. And she had nothing against some of the musicians under contract to it. They didn't include Bob Dylan, or Randy Newman, or the fabulous Joan Baez, but never mind that. What, however, were they doing to Victor? Exploiting his current popularity, that's what, instead of carefully nurturing him, the way she used to look after the musicians on the Bandiera Rossa label. Critical involvement, intervention if necessary, and always with the golden rule in mind: no disk at all is better than a bad disk. In return, unconditional solidarity even when things weren't going so well. She had only to think of that Romanian—what was his name again? When the fashion for gypsy jazz faded, she'd found him a job as a caretaker. Well, otherwise he'd have had to go back to

Romania. But this world's not about to stop turning for want of ingratitude. The Romanian simply went off to another record company with his new songs, which had nothing whatever to do with the music that had made him successful. They were crude, rhythmically insecure, hopelessly kitsch folk music—or whatever it was supposed to be. He was on quite the wrong track. And she'd known it too, so of course she couldn't offer an advance for something bound to fail. But of course the new record company could and did: oh yes, right away, and never mind about the artist. Then things really went downhill. The Romanian's CD sold fantastically well, so now he performed nothing but kitsch. What a disaster! Today his CDs sold all over the world, he gave concerts in America and so on. But the artist in him? Dead. And once again, did he think of being grateful to her? Not likely. Or was it too much to ask to expect him to say in his interviews who really gave him his start and was still selling his early CDs?

Frau Radek limped into the little park on Bayerischer Platz and decided to have a rest. She sat down on a bench and watched a group of shaven-headed lads drinking beer and kicking up a racket. They weren't worried about war so long as something, anything was going on. If she took off her glasses she couldn't see any difference between them and Victor's band. Even where their singing was concerned. She'd made Victor an offer: come to Bandiera Rossa, you won't find a better producer and manager anywhere, or one who'll take more of the work off your shoulders, and meanwhile you can get a proper training at the Conservatory. But he didn't want to. Even when she faced him with the facts: he was going to his ruin, he hadn't a ghost of a chance as an untrained musician of twenty without any diploma, he was no genius and no one was waiting to snap up musicians like him, life and the world were cruel, enemies and the envious were lying in wait everywhere, and by the age of thirty at the most, when the charms of youth were gone, he'd be out on the street, destitute and without a future. And strictly speaking she had been right. That's to say, at thirty he had been *artistically* destitute and without a future. Not exactly out on the street, no, but she rather doubted whether those luxury hotels where his record company always put him up were good for such an immature character. That was why he thought himself someone, why he believed he could dispense with his mother's advice and help. Yet who knew her way around the music business as well as she did? Twenty-eight years in it! She knew what she was talking about. And she wanted only the best for her son, unlike the head of his record company. That was why she'd had to write the man a frank letter. Whereupon Victor broke off all contact with her, which was a blow, yes, but what wouldn't she do to protect her child from danger? (And there hadn't been so very much contact between them before.) Yet there was really nothing much in that letter, just a few perfectly normal remarks, the kind you sometimes dropped in the music business, on the top level where people all knew each other. That was why she'd been so disappointed when the head of the record company told Victor about the letter. Couldn't you trust anyone these days? And all that fuss just because, with the interests of her son's career at heart, she had advised them not to issue any more of Victor's CDs for the time being, because their musical craftsmanship was so bad that his reputation would soon be permanently damaged. Well, she was right! And she'd imagined it all so nicely: she'd take Victor out into the country somewhere and help him to recover his self-confidence, they'd sit down together and finally discuss everything that had gone wrong between them these last few years, and in the end they'd begin working on a new CD. It would have got Victor away from that Natasha for a while, too. She was incredible, that little bit of fluff. Just because her lord and master wouldn't speak to his mother anymore at that time, Natasha suddenly went all monosyllabic on the phone. Could you imagine it these days? No independence, no feminine solidarity. And how could a girl like that help Victor? Very likely she thought him brilliant if he only whistled a nursery rhyme. In addition, Natasha was so hardhearted that she wouldn't give her the slightest information about her son, saying she'd better ask Victor himself. How stupid! *Ask Victor himself*—when he wasn't speaking to her!

Frau Radek rose from the park bench and hobbled on. Beyond the park she turned into a residential street. She had been to look at a one-bedroom apartment there six months ago, just after Victor bought the house in Paris. For it had occurred to her at the time, why did she need her apartment with its five rooms when she could move into a couple of rooms in Victor's house, which would mean she wouldn't be in Berlin so very often anyway. That had been soon after Victor's phone call. No word from him for two years, and then all of a sudden, "I hear you're giving up the shop?" There, she'd thought, you never would admit it, but mine isn't just any store, it's Bandiera Rossa, and not surprisingly word gets around that I'm giving it up. "So now I expect you're sorry," she'd replied. "You could have dropped in now and then."

"Well, no, I'm not sorry. I'm only wondering what you'll do without the shop."

"Oh, don't let that worry you. I have any number of plans. Maybe I'll learn the guitar and make a CD of my own . . ."

She had laughed a little, but of course she meant it seriously.

"Hm," was all Victor replied, but she knew that had impressed him. After all, it was quite something: his old mother showing everyone how it should be done. She had some good ideas for lyrics too. And melodies—well, twenty-eight years in daily contact with music and her customers, she knew better than anyone what it takes to make people tap their feet. Victor would be looking around for work yet. Perhaps that was why he reacted with such reserve. Competition from the top, so to speak.

"Well, that's okay, then. I thought you might be broke."

"Broke? Me?" she laughed again. "You'd like that, wouldn't you?"

"What? No. It wouldn't really bother me either way. It's just that Natasha thought . . . oh, very well."

He sounded exhausted. Probably because of Natasha. She was an exhausting young woman. No doubt that was why he was calling: he was at his wit's end, and who do you turn to then? To the person closest to you, of course. All the same, she wasn't going to go along with him just yet; after all, it was nearly two years since he'd been in touch.

As casually as possible, she said, "I thought maybe if my shop went bust you'd see it as the triumph over me that you've obviously been wanting for years."

"Oh . . ." Victor's voice retreated. "Well, if you want a word with her . . ."

"Now, now, don't go running away again, Victor! You have to face your problems! Victor!"

". . . Hello?"

What did *she* want? "Hello, Natasha. It's a long time since we spoke." Keep it friendly. She wasn't showing any weakness to Natasha.

"Well, it's all a bit difficult."

Difficult? What was so difficult about Victor and Natasha quarreling? These things happened from time to time. But a little bit of fluff like that probably thought right away that it was the end of the world.

"Well, you see, I've known Victor a little longer than you . . . It's all perfectly normal."

"Ah. Well, anyhow it seems you're not in such a bad way after all."

"In a bad way? What about?"

"Well, because of the shop. It was your life."

"But my dear girl! My life is so full—the shop was only one important part of it. But there are many other important things in my life, and now I have time for them at last. I don't know if you can understand that."

Natasha sighed. She was always sighing. Such a die-away air. She'd have liked to say: have a bit more fun, girl! Enjoy life! Show a little more power. Look at me. You won't keep Victor for long with that eternal martyred look, I can assure you.

"Understand? I'm trying to," replied Natasha. "Did Victor tell you we've bought a house in Paris?"

For a moment her breath was taken away. "You've done what?"

"What do you mean?"

"You've bought a house? In Paris? Who's going to pay for it?"

"Well . . . it's already paid for."

"Already paid for!" For God's sake—Victor! *We've bought a house*, indeed. They must be joking! Who had the money for that kind of thing? That bloodsucker Natasha? With the meager salary from her job as an attorney? An attorney representing asylum seekers! Oh yes, that must be bringing in the money! More than enough to buy houses in Paris, she was sure!

"So how about later?" she asked.

"What do you mean, later?"

"When there's no more money! Paris is anything but cheap! And then again, if you two split up who does the house belong to?"

"Listen, I was really going to invite you to come and spend a few days with us, just try it out, see if perhaps we can't establish something like a civilized relationship. But if that's how you feel . . ."

There she went again! Hardhearted, unfeeling!

"I suppose as a mother I'm allowed to worry! After all, it's Victor's future at stake."

"If that's how you want it. Could you just think whether you'd like to . . . well, maybe visit us for the weekend? I'll give you our number here . . ."

So it was before she'd gone to Paris that she looked at the one-bedroom apartment.

Frau Radek reached Tauentzienstrasse. It was very busy. The stores were full to bursting. All this conspicuous consumption. People thought of nothing but spending money. In times like these, too! Very likely no one was thinking about New York. Frau Radek hobbled toward the Memorial Church, casting bitter glances at the people coming toward her with a particularly large number of shopping bags. And it had been the same in Paris. Consumption, consumption, consumption. Natasha, for instance. She hadn't noticed it so much before, but there in Paris—all the girl could do was go shopping. Dragging her around from store to store, to find her a better pair of shoes, indeed! Because apparently she'd complained of her hip. First, she never complained, and second, what happened three months later? She had to have an operation, that's what. And then to be accused of complaining! And when, after the hundredth store, she said in friendly tones, "Why don't we sit down in a nice quiet café and talk about what happens next?" she was told, "There's nothing for us to talk about." And a woman like that claimed she wanted to find her a better pair of shoes. Cold and calculating. There, Victor, see how well I'm looking after your mother? But Natasha was mainly trying on shoes herself the whole time. No doubt that was the only reason she went with her. And Victor pretending he had work to do! He'd had work to do ever since she arrived. Natasha probably made a scene every evening: you're not to gang up with your mother against me! Although the house was not small (there'd even have been three rooms for her, but she didn't need that much space), she'd been able to hear them quarreling. She couldn't hear exactly what it was about, but Natasha had told Victor at least twice to be a little nicer. He must be making Natasha feel very much *de trop* just now. It was Natasha, again, who started that scene in the evening, though all had been peace and calm up till then. She herself had praised the house at length over supper, even if, as she said, "Well, it's not really in Paris itself." In the suburbs, yes, and very attractive, but not in Paris.

"We were really looking for something in the country. Nothing but countryside all around . . . and then someone told us about this place, and I immediately fell in love with the house," said Victor.

Why did he speak with such constraint? Weren't the three of them alone together? More or less. Was he afraid of his Natasha, maybe? Was she jealous?

"Oh, well, I only thought, if I were to stay rather longer—I have this hip trouble, you know—and then if I have to go to the doctor, of course the doctor will be in Paris . . ."

Why were they looking at her like that?

"But apart from that, Paris is really wonderful. And I'd like to thank you again, Natasha, for our lovely outing today."

Oh, she wasn't born yesterday! She wasn't about to provide any excuse for a quarrel.

"I'm glad you liked it," said Natasha.

"Paris is a city I could really get used to."

But as neither of them said anything to that, and after all, she had her own pride, she went on to talk about the museums, exhibitions, and other sights she wanted to see in Paris. And then they all had a nice conversation, because she knew more about the subject than they did. The two of them didn't seem a bit interested in the city, although they lived on its outskirts. "What, you don't know?" It kept slipping out. But if they really didn't . . . ! Unfortunately they all kept drinking more and more wine, and also unfortunately Natasha didn't tolerate it well. Because when the point came where she herself returned to the subject by just saying, all sassy and straight out, "Well, so how many rooms were you planning to give me?" Natasha stood up and said flatly: "You two had better settle this between you." Well! She thought

Natasha and Victor were supposed to be a couple. And with all three of them together they were almost a family. Hadn't she spent all day with Natasha? Buying shoes? Almost like best friends. And now? She for one didn't think it right to discuss the matter alone with Victor. He was acting rather oddly this evening, she thought. It was probably the wine.

"Oh, do stay, Natasha. After all, it affects all three of us."

"I have some phone calls to make. And what's more, I'm tired of acting as a buffer for you, just because you're afraid of talking to Victor on his own."

And with that nonsensical remark Natasha disappeared. It was the craziest thing she'd ever heard. And Victor seemed odder all the time; he was drinking only water now, as if afraid of losing control of himself. To defuse the situation she said, "There now, Victor, do tell me what you're working on so hard at the moment. We haven't discussed that at all."

"Listen, you don't seriously think you can stay here any longer, do you?"

"I beg your pardon?"

"All that stuff you were spouting—what did you mean?"

"Please, Victor, not in that tone of voice!"

"We invited you for three days. And that's something, after the last two years. Let's see how things go, and maybe you'll come again some time."

"Maybe? Some time? Victor, I'm an old woman. As you see, I can hardly walk."

"Then try to behave so that people don't keep wanting to throw you out of the window."

"*You* telling *me* how to behave? I'll die laughing!"

"Go ahead."

"Victor, you may not realize it, but if you carry on like this you're going straight to your ruin."

"Indeed."

"You can't just drive your mother out."

Ah, now he was rubbing his forehead in desperation. Perhaps he was finally seeing the light.

But then he said, "I'm only asking you to be as friendly and maybe companionable as if you were one of our neighbors. That's all I want. Let's talk about the weather and what to plant in the garden, and maybe you'd like to bake a cake or something—but as for anything else, forget it!" And he rose to his feet and cleared the plates away in silence.

Talk about the weather, bake a cake—what did he take her for? She, who for twenty-eight years had run a politically committed record shop . . . but suddenly she didn't want to think of that anymore. So it had come to this: her own son refused to recognize all she had done, all she'd learned, all she had experienced in life, and was shunting her off into the silly-old-lady category. It couldn't be true . . .

Victor had put the dishes in the sink, and went to the door. "It would be nice if you could take in what I just said. Good night."

And he left her alone. As usual. She said quietly, to the door, "Good night." No answer but silence. Dear God, did she feel sad! And small. And cheated by life. If anyone could have seen her—tears sprang from her eyes at the mere idea. The person she loved most, for whom she'd done everything, to whom she'd give anything—that person, her son, felt like throwing her out of the window. Was this the lesson she must learn: However hard you tried, however well you meant, however brave you were, in the end you were repaid only with contempt and death? Because she'd certainly die soon. She didn't want to go on any longer. Not any longer. More wine. There was still a full bottle left. It wouldn't make any difference. She might as well be drunk. No one would bother. You came into the world alone and you went out of it alone. So much for her visit to her son and his girlfriend in Paris! All those things she'd imagined in the plane. Breakfast together in the Champs-Elysées, a boat trip on the Seine, conversations clearing everything up, new understanding, new insights, plans, making friends with Natasha—yes, perhaps even baking a cake, why not, if the rest went well? For instance, if Victor could forgive her. She knew she had her weaknesses. Too dominant, too forthright. But she'd had to struggle all her life to make her way, that left its mark on you, it toughened you up, surely Victor must see that. And then perhaps he could pass over this or that little slip of hers with a bantering remark. The way you do among friends . . . . Oh no, what nonsense—she thought she was tough, did she? Compared to those two she was the original sensitive plant. Look at the way they treated other people! Her second evening in Paris, and they left her all on her own! In this kitchen with the peeling plaster on its walls, in she had no idea what suburb! She wasn't going to start on again about her son and her sort-of daughter-in-law—but no distant acquaintance would treat you like that. She ought really to leave at once. Suppose she went into Paris? She could afford a smart hotel. Wouldn't they just be surprised! A five-star or six-star hotel, a however-many-stars there were hotel. Why not? Wasn't she worth it? And couldn't she afford it? Yes, that was what she'd do: call a taxi, she'd find one somewhere, and then phone tomorrow and say, quite casually, Well, I thought it would be nice to see a little more of Paris, wouldn't you like to come and have lunch on the balcony here? There's a fantastic view.

And that was exactly what she had done.

Frau Radek hobbled over the forecourt of the Memorial Church. She would soon reach the Kempinski Hotel. Better sit down for awhile on the bench here. Have a little rest, collect her thoughts—after all, she needed to concentrate hard on what she was going to say to Victor. Now that there was soon to be a real war they must end their personal hostilities. She just hoped he hadn't gone out. When she called reception an hour ago, he'd been there. Of course Victor would be surprised. He never could believe what good connections she had in the music business. She still had them. So it had been easy for her to find out the hotel where he was staying. Why was that man coming over to her?

"No, I do not have any spare change!"

The place was full of derelicts! Well, now she must go through everything she wanted to say to Victor again. Right, first, of course, she was sorry—no, wait—sorry? She was still dreadfully upset. How could it have happened? Luckily the fire took hold only in the kitchen and the three rooms on the floor above. And it almost caught Natasha too, except that she had to make a phone call in the middle of the night. Well, yes, presumably she'd been drunk and she didn't notice the fire on the floor below until quite late. But you'd have to have been in a coma not to notice. Never mind, she wouldn't say anything about that. Poisoning by smoke inhalation was poisoning by smoke inhalation, no question. All the same, she herself had done nothing but leave the kitchen, fetch her bag, and go out to the taxi. Yes, there were candles burning, and perhaps she had knocked against the table slightly in going out, she'd been so furious, but she hadn't seen anything, let alone smelled it. Or if so, then she hadn't registered that something was actually burning. At most she might have thought: There's disaster brewing. And she'd always been warning them about that.

When the fairy glided over to sit on the bench beside her, Frau Radek was just thinking that their insurance had met the entire damage, so if you looked at it that way . . .

"Good evening, I am a fairy and I've come to grant you a wish."

"What?" Frau Radek reluctantly turned her head.

"I am a fairy and I've come—"

"A fairy?" What was all this nonsense? Frau Radek looked the creature beside her up and down. One of the derelicts? A clean dress, all the same—but what did that mean? No shoes? In fact, nothing on under the dress at all. Barefoot? Probably some kind of sect. That was all she needed. "Are you trying to fool me? I may be getting on a bit, but I'm not witless. And no, I do not have any spare change. What's more, God knows I have more important things to think about just now."

"No, please, I really am a fairy and you really can have a wish granted. The following areas are out, though: immortality, health, money, love." The fairy spoke slowly and smiled a lot. It was her first day on fairy duty, and she was afraid of doing something wrong.

"All those are out? What's left, then?"

"Oh, all sorts of things. For instance, if you want a dishwasher—"

"A dishwasher? Are you trying to be funny? I ran a left-wing record store for twenty-eight years, and I always worked before that too, and let me tell you something, I've washed dishes by hand all my life."

"It was only an example."

"Then you ought to think harder about your examples. Because that was no example, it was an insult."

She was getting rather worked up, but just as well. If she let off steam now she'd be all the more casual with Victor later.

"I only wanted to—" the fairy said, trying to retrieve her mistake. But she could get no further.

"First: you should never *only* want something. And second, I thought you said you were a fairy. Then you must know a few things about human beings. Offering a woman like me a dishwasher makes a mockery of her whole life. As if I could wish for nothing more important."

"I see," said the fairy. "I'm sorry. Just wish for what you want."

"Well, yes, what else did you have in mind? Wishing for what *you* want, perhaps? Don't make me laugh."

The fairy thought it better to say no more for the moment. She hovered motionless beside the woman with the thick-lensed black sunglasses, and hoped that this client's wish could be quickly granted.

"What made you come to me anyway?"

The fairy explained the system, and said that Frau Radek had obviously wished for something during the last few days.

"Yes, I'm sure I wished for all sorts of things. Wishes are all I have left to me."

"You see? Now you can have one of them granted if you tell me what it is."

"Aha."

The fairy was slightly surprised to see that the woman received this unexpected gift as a matter of course, and even seemed cross about it. But she didn't know much about human reactions yet. This morning, for instance, a man had burst into tears of joy, and his wish had just been for his girl-friend to have missed a flight in the USA three days ago. Funny, that.

"And it will truly be granted?"

Frau Radek didn't really believe what the barefoot girl was saying, but on the other hand, if it was the truth, it would be stupid to pass up this chance. Today of all days. She had nothing to lose. And she didn't have to think long about her wish. It had been the same for years: she wanted Victor to understand who was closest to him in the whole world, who really wanted to help him.

"If it's within the rules."

"Very well, then pay attention: I want my son finally to understand what I mean to him."

The fairy heaved a silent sigh of relief. That one was possible.

"And your wish is granted."

IN THE VALLEY OF DEATH

Horst strode to the doorway and folded his arms. Tangled hair hung over his forehead, and his fevered eyes flashed dangerously. A menacing growl emerged from the depths of his throat. There he stood, like an avenger sent from God, and the soldiers bent beneath his gaze like young plum trees bowing to the biting Adriatic wind.

"You shall not pass!" Horst hurled his challenge at them. "Only over my dead body!"

But he had reckoned without the Colonel. First he heard only the hard, heavy tread approaching from the other end of the hut, then the group of soldiers parted, and the Colonel stepped up to Horst, a cigarette between his fingers. He drew on the cigarette one last time before dropping it to the ground and then, with a thin, contemptuous smile, treading it out. Only now did he look Horst in the eye.

"So you want to prevent your comrades from doing their duty?" In spite of his mighty stature the Colonel had a high, effeminate voice that certain comics among the soldiers always made the butt of their jokes.

"I want to prevent them from committing a crime."

"You call it a crime to smoke out a partisans' camp?"

"They're not partisans, they're simple peasants."

"Indeed?" The Colonel's hand went to his pistol pocket. Without taking his eyes off Horst, he undid the button and took out the pistol. "Because maybe partisans wouldn't want one of their women fucking a German soldier? Is that your proof?"

Horst could have strangled the Colonel with his bare hands. He wasn't having anyone speaking of Oksana in such terms.

"You can shoot me, but you can't speak to me like that!"

The Colonel uttered a laugh as high and womanish as his voice. "And who, may I ask, is going to stop me?"

"It may not be today, it may not be tomorrow, but some day I'll crush you like a worm."

The Colonel turned to the soldiers on his right and left, grinning. "All this for a partisan whore! Just because he's fucking a Yugoslav tart!"

At the same moment Horst leaped at him, but that was what the Colonel had just been waiting for. "Take that, you bastard!" he shouted, and shot Horst in the legs.

Peter Ohio—his pseudonym; his real name was Rudolf Kratzer—put the two sheets of paper down on his desk and leaned back in his chair. "Pure crap," he said out loud to himself. How many times had he written that scene now? And he still couldn't get it right. *Plum trees in the biting Adriatic wind*— what tripe! And up to this point he'd thought the novel was going rather well. Arrival in Serbia, first military operations, meeting Oksana at the well, the secret rendezvous, mental conflict beginning to rear its head, sex with Oksana for the first time, tearing up Hitler's picture straight afterwards— yes, all that was great, but then suddenly here he was again: *The Black Colonel in the Valley of Death*.

In 1954 Rudolf Kratzer had sent his first novel, *The Black Colonel Never Gives Up*, to several publishing firms. One of them replied, recommending him to try the kind of firm that published pulp fiction for station bookstalls. With some distaste—for Kratzer thought that his novel, which was told in the style of a Western, was a good, topical metaphor for the human will to survive, and thus really a book for serious publishing houses—he finally overcame his reluctance and sent the manuscript to Giselle Publishing. A week later he was asked to come and discuss it in their offices on Innsbrucker Platz. By the end of the meeting the editor in chief had persuaded him to adopt a pseudonym and sign a contract stipulating delivery of one *Colonel* novel a month for the next two years, the novels to contain as much exciting action and as few metaphors as possible. After the end of the two years, and in view of the unexpectedly great success of the *Colonel* series, Kratzer renegotiated his terms. He now had more money, more freedom to plan his storylines, more time, and the chance to write a second series, which became the famous *Alabama Snake* novels. And so the years passed by. Steady success, a good, regular salary, on one occasion a discussion of his work in a serious weekly journal under the headline: *Real Men at the Bookstall for Seventy-Five Pfennigs*, the purchase of an apartment in Charlottenburg, two weddings, one divorce, two children, a regular guest at three restaurants, vacations by Lake Constance, two trips to the U.S., membership in the American Country Club, a master's dissertation by a student of German literature on light fiction in West Germany with special reference to the novels of Peter Ohio, death of his second wife, two mistresses, chosen Author of the Month by Giselle Publishing's readers for the twenty-seventh time for *The Black Colonel in the Valley of Death*, two heart attacks, impotence. The doctor might say he had many years ahead of him yet, but he was seventy-eight and not a total fool. His life was drawing to an end, whatever the doctors said. So now, at last, he must write the story that had been preying on his mind for nearly sixty years. For he believed that he would have been happy with Oksana. And furthermore, this was his last chance to make Peter Ohio a name respected in the literary world after all.

Ohio rose from his desk and, limping slightly, went down the hall, past four other rooms, and into the kitchen to make himself a cup of tea. The apartment seemed quieter and emptier every day. In fact it was full of furniture, some of which was inherited from his grandparents, and a collection of pop art posters. The expensively framed Warhols and Lichtensteins were all propped on the floor, leaning against bookshelves and walls. He had seen this effect in a documentary film about Picasso: pictures all over the house but none of them hanging. He had begun collecting the posters some time in the seventies. At that point Ohio had hoped for a while that with the new interest certain German publishers and newspapers were taking in American crime novels and light literature, he might finally join the ranks of those authors who were taken seriously. And because the people interested in this kind of literature were mostly young and modern, he began creating himself a new lifestyle, even though he was over fifty. Instead of listening to whatever was on the radio, drinking beer, and buying naïve paintings from Lake Constance, he suddenly began going in for French chansons, jazz, white wine, and pop art. He spent a whole summer going to readings by long-haired young authors, he visited exhibitions in damp cellars where bottled beer was drunk and New York bands played, and in the evenings he went to the Charlottenburg bars frequented by students and artists. He had a three-day affair with a girl student of American literature; it lasted until he gave her one of his novels. She read half of it, told Ohio his American Indians were racist clichés, and threw him out. Other acquaintanceships that he made that summer never lasted any longer than three days either. Sometimes a discussion in a bar about comparative structures of narrative in novels and movies would go on until eight in the morning, sometimes he spent the afternoon by the lake with a group of art students, all stoned out of their minds, who kept sending him to the kiosk every half hour to buy chocolate bars and pretzels, and once he was invited to a private porn movie show, which made him, apparently unlike everyone else, feel first embarrassed and then, also apparently unlike everyone else, horny—at least, after the show they all drank tea and discussed the difference between sex and eroticism. Ohio could do what he liked: be curious, interested, serious, ironic, get drunk, stay sober, boast, talk big, listen, chauffeur people through the Berlin night in his Cadillac, stand them drinks in bars, buy pictures from young painters which his wife immediately stowed in the cellar, praise poems of which he understood nothing except that they mustn't rhyme, watch films of young people sitting on sofas, looking out of windows, and breakfasting half naked, take note of more and more new music groups, whose disks he bought and listened to in the afternoon so that he could join the discussion of them in the evening—but all the same, at the end of that summer he was still the weird old guy in cowboy boots, jeans, and denim jacket who wrote some kind of Wild West nonsense.

He put the kettle on the stove, took a teabag out of its packet, hung it in the cup and waited for the water to boil. It wasn't really quiet in the apartment either. Some kind of modern music echoed up from the floor below day in, day out, and there'd been renovations in progress on the floor above for the last three weeks. All the same: an empty, quiet apartment. Since his last mistress, Marita, moved away from Berlin, he had had exactly nine visits in four years. Four times, always at Christmas, his widowed sister came. She'd hated him ever since, in that hopeful summer in the seventies, he had described her husband, a police officer, as a Nazi and a petit bourgeois (he really did it only on account of the student of American literature, so that he could feel close to her once more; that was two weeks after she threw him out, and he hadn't seen her again). Twice he had a visit from his son, who worked as a head of department for the Karstadt chain of stores, speculated on the stock exchange as a sideline, and spent his visits sitting on the sofa following the share prices on television. Once his daughter came with her new boyfriend, about the fifth since her divorce; the boyfriend's parents had emigrated from Turkey and he kept making jokes about the Turks, which first irritated and then infuriated Peter Ohio. And finally there were two visits from the Giselle Publishing concept manager, aged thirty-one, who wanted to persuade him to lend his name to a new series written by a young team. The central character was a kind of Greenpeace version of James Bond, who in the course of the first twelve episodes turned out to be the disowned and repudiated son of an Arabian royal house. Brought up as a child by a lonely old Christian lady, he had seen so many accidents at oil wells and pipelines in his native land that when he reached twenty he decided to save the earth. Meanwhile, he appreciated good champagne and would remain a bachelor for the time being, breaking hearts but never a promise to God.

"What utter tripe!" said Ohio. "Who reads that sort of stuff today?"

"Oh, Peter!" The concept manager succeeded in giving him a smile which was both admiring and superior. "*You* may have changed, but the world hasn't. People still want this kind of thing. Come on, do yourself a favor, you'll get a quarter percent, and what do you have to lose?"

My name, Ohio almost said, but he saw the trap just in time. "You probably won't understand me, but all the same: I've been writing this stuff for forty years, and there's no realistic prospect of the name Ohio being connected with anything but cowboy adventures, but it's been my pseudonym for over forty years, and at least once I want to write a real book under it."

"Yes, of course you do. I've said so from the start: there's more to Peter Ohio than the *Colonel* novels, he'll give us a nice surprise yet. In the content of your work, I've always seen you on a par with Grass and Walser, and once you're free of the formal constraints of the Western genre . . ." The concept manager had in fact read something like this in an arts supplement, in a piece on German literature by an African writer: if you took all the posturing and the foreign words out of people like Grünbein and Walser, and gave their work a proper sentence structure instead, those German literary critics whose brains hadn't yet been entirely turned to fatty liver by the consumption of salmon canapés and white wine would see what trashy ideas it contained. Not that the concept manager had ever heard of Grünbein, but Grass was presented in an equally unflattering light elsewhere in the text. A girl intern had brought him the article, and thought it might make an ad. A quotation and then, say: "Save yourself looking up words in the dictionary—just read books from Giselle Publishing." It would never do, of course.

"But why not just write this new, different book under your real name and leave the Ohio byline to us?"

"As I said, it's my nom de plume, several of the *Colonel* and *Alabama* novels aren't at all bad, and who knows, people might reread them more attentively if they associate them with the new book. And anyway it's all part of my work."

"Of course, of course it's your work. I understand perfectly. But perhaps you should stop to think whether the name Ohio might not even be a drawback to this new book, seeing it will be so much more serious and literary? I mean, you know how superficial the book trade is, the people who set the tone could easily say: Oh, Ohio, he's the Western writer, there can't be anything in that book."

"I doubt if the people who set the tone have ever heard of Peter Ohio. And if my earlier history comes out at some point, I might even be glad."

"*Earlier* history . . . That reminds me of something quite different: Isn't it your birthday soon? Your eighty-eighth, eighty-ninth?"

"My seventy-ninth."

"Oh, sorry. Can't get my head around figures . . . Anyway, we were thinking of bringing out a special *Colonel* anthology for the occasion. Although I have to say, we did envisage it in connection with our launch of the *Genghiz* series."

Genghiz on the Track of the Killers of the Amazon—the series as a whole wasn't intended to sound very Arabian.

"In that case," said Ohio, "the answer is no."

"Ah. I see. But perhaps you'd think it over again. And do remember how long you and Giselle Publishing have been working together. It's almost like a marriage, it can't simply fall apart after all those years. What do you think?"

Ohio thought he was tired now. A week later the concept manager came back, this time with all the contracts and financial details. After Ohio had once again refused to lend his name to the Genghiz series, the concept manager pointed out how few *Colonel* and *Snake* titles had sold over the last few years.

"I know the excellent Herr Rust wrote a regular salary for life into your contract because of all you've done for the firm. But that's only—and I really do feel awkward about saying this—it's only, of course, as long as your books are in print and on the market. Our lawyer—Alex, you know him—he's looked into the matter. Well, of course the *Genghiz* series would be a great opportunity to crank up sales of the back list. I don't want to be overenthusiastic, but the first *Genghiz* episodes I read—don't take this the wrong way, but I think people will say: wow, I simply must read this author's other series too. So if we don't use this opportunity, then . . . well, I can't conjure up *Colonel* readers out of nothing."

Peter Ohio was trembling with rage and fear as he rose from the sofa and said, "But I don't want to do it. So now would you please go? I have work to do."

That had been his last visit from anyone, and in three months' time, at Christmas, his sister would probably come back.

Ohio poured boiling water over the teabag. Why couldn't he get that scene with the Colonel right? By now he was so afraid of failing that his mouth went dry at the mere thought of the scene. Suppose he tried just describing the course of events as if it were a police report? No comparisons, no imagery, no flights of fancy, however small, nothing ambitious. But then what about the literary element? The skillfully turned sentences for the reader to relish? The marginal observations that often said much more than the main narrative? The images that conveyed the sensuous experience of the story? Marita, for instance, and after all she ran the Friedenau Ecumenical Art Association, Marita had always loved his similes. *A man like one of the remaining columns of the Acropolis, weathered by the passing of centuries, yet standing straight and upright every day.* Or: *The girl leaped downhill like a little goat in love.*

"That's really good. I can see the picture in my head at once. Wherever do you get these ideas?"

She'd admired his philosophical flights of fancy too. *When at last he saw the desert before him, the Colonel thought:*

Such is life, but perhaps there'll be an oasis somewhere, and a girl in the oasis, and perhaps the girl will have room for me in her bed, and the hope of that will make me forget my thirst and my fear. And he rode confidently on. Or then again: *Snake felt his blood forming little streams around him, he saw the bound and gagged Princess Romanova at the other end of the burning hut, and he thought: Love is the only remedy for the fear of death.* (That one he'd stolen, from more than one book, and it should really say *Sex is the only remedy*, but for Giselle Publishing's readers the word was taboo in both style and content, not that Marita knew any of that, naturally.)

"Sometimes I think of you as a kind of spiritual teacher. The way you describe life is simply so . . . well, as if you were looking down from a mountain, like Moses, and you saw everything that makes human beings tick."

The bit about Moses had been slightly embarrassing, because he had a feeling she was trying to imitate him, but basically, of course, Marita's comments went down extremely well. And wouldn't she read his new novel? So would she speak in such euphoric terms if the new novel was like a police report? Not that it had anything to do with Marita. Marita had gone to live with her daughter in Canada, and they only occasionally exchanged postcards. But take her as an example. And hers weren't the only compliments on his style he'd been paid over the years. There was a carton full of fan letters on his shelves. Although he had to admit most of them were from housewives or fifteen-year-olds. And a few servicemen, night watchmen, ambulance men waiting on call, but also—at any rate—a not inconsiderable number of high school teachers.

Ohio took the teabag out of the cup and threw it in the bin. But he'd had all this appreciation for over forty years. Now he wanted to move up into a different league, and for that—he snapped the lid of the bin shut—for that those plum trees must go!

Back at his desk, he threw those two pages into the bin without even reading them. Then he put a new sheet of paper into his typewriter and began: *Horst strode to the doorway and hurled his challenge at the soldiers. "You shall not pass! Only over my dead body!"*

But now the Colonel came through another door. "So you want to prevent your comrades from doing their duty?"

"I want to prevent them from committing a crime."

"You call it a crime to smoke out a partisans' camp?"

"They're not partisans, they're simple peasants."

"Indeed?" The Colonel's hand went to his pistol pocket. "Because maybe partisans wouldn't want one of their women fucking a German soldier? Is that your proof?"

Horst could have strangled the Colonel. He wasn't having anyone speaking of Oksana in such terms.

"You can shoot me, but you can't speak to me like that!"

"And who, may I ask, is going to stop me?"

"It may not be today, it may not be tomorrow, but some day I'll crush you like a worm."

The Colonel grinned. "All this for a partisan whore! Just because he's fucking a Yugoslav tart!"

At the same moment Horst leaped at him, but that was what the Colonel had just been waiting for.

"Take that, you bastard!"

Ohio leaned back. He was sweating, and when he read the page through his heart pounded. He liked the last bit. No shots, so the reader would be kept waiting in suspense until the next chapter to find out what had happened. But the rest of it . . . in the past he'd always been able rely on his dialogue, but somehow it didn't seem right here. *Crush you like a worm*—that was pure *Alabama Snake* style. Still, *fuck* and *tart*, he'd never written anything as authentic as that before. It was the way soldiers talked. Or did they? He hadn't mingled with soldiers for over fifty years. Well, it wasn't likely that anyone would doubt its authenticity. What else? *But now the Colonel came through another door*—probably the most boring way he'd ever described a dramatic entrance before. That sentence could be cut too. His new readership would realize that when the Colonel said something he *must* have come in. There remained the question of Oksana's innocence. Horst could be rather more indignant about that. As he had been.

Ohio sipped his tea. Had he really been much more indignant, or maybe less? Why hadn't he just warned her? Because the order to 'smoke out' the camp came as such a surprise, of course, but all the same . . . he could have guessed it was coming, something like that was in the air, no question. But his hope that nothing would happen overcame his sense of reality. Oksana . . . they'd discussed it all, in detail:

going to America after the war, California, their own house, children, travel, success. He'd already tried his hand at writing, he'd imagined the way it would all sound even better in English. And Oksana just wanted to be with him. Not like his wives later, who were always demanding "self-realization" and "my own role," and wanted to "be someone in my own right," but ended up with Spanish classes and new sofa cushions. Until impotence struck he had regularly thought about Oksana at intimate moments. She for one never had any difficulties with orgasm. When he thought of his second wife—that was the drawback of the seventies, all of a sudden people conducted such conversations even over breakfast. Oksana, on the other hand, had been full of fun, and as sensuous as if she personally had invented love. And so she had, at least for him.

What about *no* dialogue? The whole scene just a kind of nightmare sequence? In retrospect, when it was all over? Horst on his camp bed, wounded, in feverish delirium, the reader thinks: how lucky, he's just having delusions, but then it turns out to be true? Make this the only chapter in the first person, maybe? Using only indirect speech? *I stepped into the doorway and hurled a challenge at them, said they would not pass . . .they would not pass, only over . . .*

Or *only* dialogue. Like a radio play. After all, the preceding chapters made the state of mind of all involved perfectly clear. But it was the dialogue that was giving him trouble. Or tell it from the nurse's point of view? *How he tosses and turns in his fever, she thought. And what on earth was he talking about? Stepping into the doorway and hurling a challenge at them: only over his dead body . . .*

Ohio shook his head. None of it would do. He must take a more fundamental approach. If this central scene didn't work then perhaps the structure of the whole novel was wrong. It wouldn't be right even at the beginning, and it would be wrong at the end too. Ohio closed his eyes and tried to picture the rhythm of the novel as an irregular curve. Introduction of the main character, beginning of the action, rising slightly first, then more and more steeply to the climax, the curve falls away, finally there's a short, quiet, wise afterthought. So far so good, very good, but when Ohio opened his eyes and for the hundredth time began to read *Horst stepped into the doorway* he could have flung himself out of the window.

The fairy found Ohio with his arms across the desk, his head laid sideways on them, eyes closed, his lips silently forming words of some kind. She leaned forward.

"Hello?"

Without changing position, Ohio opened his eyes and looked at the fairy unmoved. In his mind he had just thrown away a hundred and thirty pages and composed the opening sentences of the novel in line with his entirely new idea of it. An unexpected visitor, however she had entered the apartment, could hold no terrors for him.

"Who are you, and what do you want?"

"I am a fairy and I've come to grant you a wish."

Ohio slowly sat up and rubbed his forehead. "Very original. Did Giselle Publishing send you? Are you supposed to offer me money? Forget it. I have enough, and I won't be needing it much longer anyway. How did you get in, by the way?"

"Through the door."

"Ah, I must have left it unlocked. You'll catch a cold in just that dress."

"We don't get such things."

"You don't get to wear a jacket? Mister Concept Manager lays down the law on clothing, does he? Do the ladies in his office have to run around half naked?"

"Colds. We fairies don't catch colds. I really am a fairy, and your door was locked."

The fairy waited until Ohio's face finally showed surprise, and then began to explain. After she had concluded her patter with the usual: "The following areas are out, though: immortality, health, money, love," Ohio scrutinized her in silence for a while. The fairy naturally thought this was an expression of amazement. In fact Ohio was wondering whether he could tell his story by bringing a fairy into it.

"So now?"

"Now you tell me your wish."

In view of the difficulty he was having with the novel, all this struck Ohio as rather stupid, but perhaps, he thought, something could be made of it. "Suppose I wished to write a really great and generally acclaimed novel some day?"

He looked a little ironic at first, as much as to say: How about that, then? But the longer the fairy took to reply the more seriously he took the situation. He began fidgeting uneasily with his teacup.

The fairy didn't know much about books, but in the past she had enjoyed going to concerts, and as far as she remembered it was rather tricky being great and at the same time generally acclaimed. A piece of music might touch her heart more deeply than she thought anyone ever had, and it meant nothing to her friend but a reason to make advances to some man standing about looking particularly bored. However, her friend tore off half her clothes and howled emotionally at a Sting concert. They often argued about which was the best music group, but they might just as well have tried to agree on the perfect man. On the other hand, they both knew such groups as the Beatles were generally acclaimed, but neither had ever heard them.

So the fairy finally asked: "Is there any such thing?"

"What?"

"Any such thing as a great *and* generally acclaimed novel. I mean with music, for instance, it's like this: one person loves a song, or, if you like, thinks it's great, another person likes something else. I mean, it's not like mathematics or the high jump."

"Well . . . !" Amused, Ohio gave a little cough. This young lady was talking nonsense. "You surely don't doubt that Goethe, for instance, is one of the most important of writers, and popular too."

"No idea, never read him, but the way a friend of mine saw it, the most important writer was the one who wrote up celebrities' parties in the magazines she reads. He was really amusing. Anyway, you'll have to clarify your wish a little. Because I can assure you, something will have to go. Either the 'great' or the 'generally acclaimed' or the 'novel.' We do grant wishes but we can't rearrange the world."

"But that's . . ." Ohio shook his head. He had never heard anything like this before. "Perhaps you didn't understand what I mean by 'generally acclaimed.' To be honest, I'm not so bothered about someone like your friend. I'm thinking of the literary world, the really important people, the arts supplements, television . . ."

"Oh, I see." The fairy, bored, looked away. "You want to be on the talk shows."

"That too," replied Ohio, in some annoyance. "But I have the whole literary scene in mind."

"Well, fine, but I can't promise that your novel will be popular as well. With human beings, I mean. And whether a literary scene can love something—in this case I don't know enough about it. But just as you like."

"Wait a moment!" Ohio felt slightly alarmed. "Of course I want to be popular with readers too."

"All of them?"

"As many as possible."

"There was a feature in a little box in my friend's magazine: This Week's Good Deed. Dogs who'd rescued someone and so on. We both liked reading that."

"Are you trying to be funny?"

"Oh no, not at all. But it's my job to get your wish defined as precisely as possible, to avoid disappointment when it's granted. Although I'll be frank with you: disappointments are always possible."

"What does that mean?"

"Like I said: we don't rearrange the world and we respect its laws. For instance, if you wished to bring out the hottest pop CD of the year, I can tell you in advance you won't be the lead singer. And if you wish to be the lead singer it won't be the hottest CD. It's that simple."

"Thank you. A telling example."

"I only wanted to make it clear. Wishes are like life: the higher you reach the further you can fall. At least, in my experience people always do best with wishes within the bounds of their own possibilities."

Ohio looked down at a Lichtenstein sunrise. The fairy was right about something, but about exactly what? He had certainly never met anyone else who didn't immediately know what "a great, generally acclaimed novel" meant. Although . . . yes, Marita and he had liked very different books. Instead of Thomas Mann and Hermann Hesse, who to Ohio were unapproachable deities, Marita adored the best-selling writer Hera Lind—she adored Ohio too, but that didn't really count. Suppose they were all of equal value in the end? Could you say Marita had no right to be more moved by Hera Lind than *Der Steppenwolf*? Then again, there were people like the concept manager who read in the paper that a certain novel was a masterpiece, and believed it and passed the word on, and ultimately helped an author to get famous enough to be recognized by taxi drivers. But—and this was the first time he had so consciously asked the question—but where should he start? Whose expectations did he want to satisfy? And did he know what anyone's expectations were like? He had never understood what Marita saw in Hera Lind. Any more than she could share his love of Hermann Hesse. She had described Hesse's books as schoolyard kitsch —and that from a woman who read Hera Lind! It all left him at a loss. And if for a moment he forgot about the fairy and the temptation to ask for a miracle, there was only one thing he'd wished for these last few days: to get that scene with the Colonel written.

The fairy cleared her throat as politely as possible. "So perhaps it's about time we . . ."

"Hm." Ohio's eyes were still lowered. He did not feel quite certain yet. Until ten minutes ago he had never questioned the standards of the literary world. What was in, what was out, what was important, unimportant, good, bad—he didn't have to think long about it. Or even briefly. And at the same time his assessment of his own works, he thought, had always been very realistic. But now? If he took what the fairy said seriously . . . after all, he'd sold several million copies, he'd helped people in the U-Bahn, in waiting rooms, in retirement homes to pass the time pleasantly, he'd been loved by several women for what he wrote, he'd had letters from readers telling him that the first thing they did at the beginning of the month was rush to the bookstall, and saying how the Colonel or Alabama Snake gave them the courage to face daily life, and all things considered he could look back on a career that was full of touching moments when perfect strangers had said he gave them hours of pleasure. So why should he, of all people, wish to write a great and generally acclaimed novel?

Ohio looked up. "To be honest, you had me a little confused."

"That does tend to happen with our visits. But don't worry too much. Less usually depends on a wish than people think."

"Right." Ohio shook himself. "I've been working on a scene in my book for over a week without getting anywhere. I wish to find the right tone and narrative viewpoint for it."

Ohio looked expectantly at the fairy.

The fairy smiled. "And your wish is granted."

I was sitting on the bed when the Colonel's order echoed down the corridor: "All men to report at once!" At first I thought it was for the usual sort of stupid reason. Cleaning out the barracks yet again, even though we'd be leaving in a few days anyway, or perhaps someone had stolen a sausage from the kitchen like last week, and the Colonel wanted to repeat his detective act in front of us again. So I wasn't bothered, even though his voice sounded as if the Red Army flags were already flapping in his face. But then Heinrich came rushing into the room and cried: "Shit, he wants to flatten the village!"

"What?"

"Seems like some partisans blew up one of our convoys last night. Now it's reprisals all over the place."

"But what does the village have to do with it?" My heart began racing.

"Nothing, of course. Makes no difference to the top brass."

"But we must stop it! This mustn't happen!"

"What?" Heinrich, who was just putting on his jacket, stopped for a moment and looked at me with amusement and a touch of sympathy. "Stop it? Because of your little lovebird, I suppose? I'm not going to ask for trouble. We'll be out of here at the end of this week, and that will be that. If I were you I'd start forgetting the girl right now. It's only an affair."

"Only an affair?" I could have struck him. He went on buttoning his jacket and picked up his gun.

"Heinrich, please! If we all refuse he can't do anything!"

"Refuse? Are you crazy? You know what'll happen then. And . . . ," here Heinrich lowered his voice, "and the war will soon be over anyway. I'm not running any more risks."

"Oh, so you would run risks if it was going to last another ten years, would you?"

"Don't shout like that, for God's sake! Suppose the Colonel hears you?"

"Answer my question!"

"Answer mine first: Why should we risk our lives just so

that you . . ." And he waggled his pelvis back and forth, grinning. Next moment I was on my feet punching him in the face. *"You stupid asshole!"* I heard him say, and then I was out of the room and racing to the barracks yard.

The first men were already lined up in rank and file, and the Colonel had begun giving orders. When he saw me rushing out of the building he fell silent and put his right hand to his pistol pocket.

"Well now, Kratzer," he said when I stood in front of him, gasping for breath. "Pleased to see you so keen to go into action."

"You can't . . . ," I fought for air and tried to speak calmly, "you can't do this. They're only peasants."

"Oh yes? Only peasants. And even if that made any difference—how come you know so much about it?"

"I've been there on reconnaissance a few times."

The Colonel turned to the men behind me. "Ah, so they call it reconnaissance these days!" And the soldiers dutifully chuckled.

"Please . . . that has nothing to do with it. I'm quite sure there isn't a single partisan down there. And," I said, looking the Colonel as straight in the eye as I could, "we'll be retreating soon anyway."

He stopped short, then his gaze suddenly turned icy. "So what does that mean: we'll be retreating soon anyway?"

"I mean . . ." I said, feeling a tic begin around my eyes, "I mean it wouldn't be right."

"Who says? The Führer? Or were you thinking, Kratzer, there could soon be other authorities you must answer to?"

I quickly shook my head. "Of course we're going to win the war."

"*Of course.*" *He slowly unbuttoned his pistol pocket.* "*With or without you. I suppose you know the penalty for refusing to obey orders?*"

"*Please. . . !*"

He grasped his pistol. "*Go get your gun now. I'll expect you here in two minutes' time.*"

I stared at him.

"*Go on!*"

Slowly, I turned and staggered back to the house.

"*And don't go thinking you can smuggle anyone out of that village. Over a hundred of our comrades were blown sky-high yesterday because of those bastards. Which means reprisals down to the very last inhabitant!*"

Heinrich was coming down the corridor toward me. He was still rubbing his nose. All the same, he stopped and whispered, "*Don't do anything stupid. If you go along with this I promise I'll try to help you hide the girl in a cupboard somewhere.*"

"*And what about her brothers and sisters, her parents, her friends? We were going to America together!*"

"*Oh, shut your trap! America! America will be coming to us soon enough. And bawling won't help you now.*"

I staggered on.

"*Rudi!*"

"*Yes, yes, with you in a minute.*"

Back in the room, I took my pistol and shot myself in the leg so that it would look like an accident.

HAPPY ENDING

Manuel was sitting at the bar of the Fôret Rieder on the Gendarmenmarkt around eleven-thirty in the morning when the door opened, and four men of about thirty wearing pale, lightweight suits came through the porch. The Fôret Rieder, an expensive restaurant and bar that had been popular with the high society of Berlin for the last two months, opened at eleven, and so far Manuel was the only guest. At this time of day he had been hoping for a little private chat with Fanny, the owner and land-lady, but unfortunately Fanny was busy ordering supplies. Or at least so she had said when Manuel steered his way to the bar on the dot of eleven with a boisterous, "Hail Fanny, those who are about to die salute you!" Manuel liked to make such remarks, which he considered an intelligent mixture of irony, erudition, and cryptic reference to the current situation, but they often merely baffled his audience.

"Oh, hi, Manuel, I just have to go into the kitchen, deal with some orders," said Fanny, stammering slightly. She closed the till and turned to the kitchen door.

"I saw outside that you're serving oysters today," Manuel forged ahead, speaking to Fanny's back, "and I said to myself: Oysters at this time of year, is the Caesar of our favorite restaurant planning to kill us all? Because the gladiators used to call themselves those who were about to die— get it?"

Fanny was already halfway through the swing doors when she turned back. "Yes, sure, very amusing. Listen, we're not too well organized yet. If you want something to drink you'll have to wait a bit."

"That's no problem. Don't you worry about me, I have plenty to do." With a brief, exaggerated expression of exhaustion Manuel indicated the full briefcase in front of him. "You deal with your orders or we'll all be wandering around like in Beckett. Because your food is our Godot."

Fanny nodded faintly. "Hmhm," she said, and looked at Manuel for a moment with mingled perplexity and concern. Manuel had taken to visiting the Fôret Rieder every other day, and the entire staff dreaded his witty sayings and his attempts to get into conversation with someone, anyone. He was a pain in the neck, they treated him like one, and Fanny longed for the day when he would realize how they felt and find another restaurant.

Manuel watched the doors swing back and forth after Fanny had gone through them, smiled to himself, and thought: wonderful woman, dry humor, never wastes a word, knows her way around. For what was her reaction to his remark about Godot but subtle, amused understanding on a very high intellectual plane? That was why he felt so much at ease in the Fôret Rieder. Good food, good wines, distinguished guests at all the tables—a real find! What he liked was the atmosphere: educated, intelligent, but perfectly normal. Yet Fanny could reasonably enough have put on a few airs; half the government came here to eat these days. But no: she'd stayed perfectly normal. A pity she wasn't his type or . . . well, perhaps even so . . .

Manuel waited for the four young men to choose a table by the window and make for it, talking cheerfully. Only then did he raise his eyes from the notes spread out in front of him and look at them with the disapproving expression of one whose private business has been disturbed.

" . . . So then I told him she was my secretary."

"What did she do?"

"Oh, you know her! Took it all in fun, of course. But the problem was that he didn't know who she was, in fact he'd never seen her before, so he simply believed all that about her being my secretary."

"No!"

"Yes, really he did."

Laughing, they pulled out the chairs and sat down.

"What line is the guy in?"

"Oh, photorealistic stuff and so on. I interviewed him once, and then he suddenly turned up at our table at the party. Nice guy, but none too bright, I guess."

"Hardly, if he doesn't even recognize the head of the team at *Art 3000*."

"Yes, but wait, here comes the real joke: I told him in a whisper a little later. Because it wasn't fair to her to leave someone at the table thinking she was a secretary. And of course I wanted to see his face too."

"Sure."

"Up till then he'd taken almost no notice of her."

"So then what? Did he make a beeline for her?"

"Well, no! That was the joke. He said: 'Oh yes?' and went on ignoring her."

"I don't believe it!"

"It's a fact. I even said it again—thought there might be some acoustic problem. But no: '*Art 3000*—oh yes?'"

"Amazing!"

"How old is he?"

"A little older than us."

"Kind of sad too."

"Well, he did know what *Art 3000* is. But all the same . . ."

At last Manuel realized why he knew the storyteller's face. He was one of the three editors in chief of what at present was the major illustrated art and fashion magazine in Germany. On the side he wrote successful books with titles like *Falling Between All Stools—German Landscape Painting From 1933 to 1945*, and *The Taboo Republic of Germany*. Manuel immediately adjusted the expression on his face and suddenly beamed at the table as if his best friends were over there, just waiting for him to join them. For Manuel was a freelance journalist. Very free at the moment, in fact. Now and then an article about his father, a well-known German architect, every few weeks an interview with his wife Sabine, the world-famous pianist—hardly anything else published these last two years. And now he was sitting less than ten meters from a man who could provide him with full employment, independent of his wife and father, just by snapping his fingers. But the longer he pictured the opportunities that a conversation with the editor in chief might open up, the more he felt the pleased expression he was bending on the four men, who ignored him completely, becoming strained. Any moment one of the four might look his way, and at that moment he must be fully in command. (Casual:) Hey, haven't we met? You're from *True, Beautiful & Good*, aren't you? A great journal. You want to know who to order from here? Personally, I always give Fanny my order. Fanny? Oh, the boss. So of course she knows better than anyone what's particularly fresh. But she's ordering at the moment herself. That's life (a little laugh): the whole world is ordering, and when the circle closes we're all left emptyhanded. (The others laugh): Who said that? Shakespeare. (They look surprised, I laugh:) No, only joking, it just slipped out. Yes, I said it myself. What do I do? I'm a journalist too. Freelance. I could never imagine working any other way. (Or no, better): Because I haven't found the right team yet. (Or better still, taking the bull by the horns—why not?—but with a twinkle in the eye:) Because of course I've been keeping myself free for *True, Beautiful & Good*. (Smiling): Of course I mean it seriously. No, I'm afraid I don't have time tomorrow,

I have to go to Hamburg. The day after tomorrow? That ought to be okay. If you'd give me the address. Fine. Well, I'll just tell Fanny you're here. But Rome wasn't built in a day—how about an aperitif first? No problem, I can get you one. Oh, this place is like a home away from home to me.

By now Manuel was staring at the men with so fixed a smile that a chance observer might have expected him to go for them any moment with an ax. Would Fanny mind if he gave the four of them a glass of champagne—to go on his bill, of course? That, he felt convinced, would mean his editorial job was more or less in the bag. And later he could always tell Fanny he'd done it only to save the restaurant's reputation: you don't keep the editors in chief of *True, Beautiful & Good* waiting so long. Suppose they took it into their heads, for instance, to write a piece slamming the service in the Fôret Rieder? These things happen. Some snotty young reporter has had a tough rump steak—quick, front page of the arts section, amusing article headlined "The Sole of a Shoe, Twenty Euros— Where the Wealthy Berliner Plays the Parisian."

Suddenly Fanny's loud laughter rang out from the kitchen, and Manuel turned to the swing door. Next moment she came through it carrying a carton, nodded briefly to him and went to the corner where the espresso machine stood. As she took coffee bags out of the carton and stacked them under the counter she looked at the men and said, "Hi, guys, someone'll be with you in a minute. We're running a little late today."

"That's no problem."

"Hey, Fanny, oysters in midsummer? Trying to poison us?"

Fanny laughed. "Don't worry. They're very fresh, arrived this morning."

As Fanny passed Manuel on her way back to the kitchen she didn't glance at him, so he could have saved himself the trouble of looking particularly uninterested. In fact there was a touch of sadness in his eyes. Okay, so he might not be one of her very top customers, but he'd made the joke first, and much more wittily. Couldn't she just have mentioned it? Manuel said that too. What Manuel? Oh, don't you know Manuel? He's in your own line of business. Manuel, would you come over here a minute? Let me introduce you to our most faithful (or: our favorite?) guest— well, I could really say friend, this is kind of your home away from home, right, Manuel?—Well, if I had a corner where I could put my computer . . . Computer? Ah, so you write too? We must have a little talk . . . Well, guys, I'll leave you to it, I must get back to the kitchen . . .

"Manuel Reuter?"

Manuel jumped. One of the four, on his way to the men's room, had stopped beside him.

"Yes . . . ?"

"Don't you remember me? The name's August. I photographed your wife last year for *stern*, and then we went for a drink."

"Oh yes, of course: August!" Manuel was trying to make the face fit some particular evening. "Sorry, I'm working on a report on, well . . ." he clicked his tongue, "on new artistic forms of expression in the Peking underground scene—it's a difficult subject, so that's why I didn't . . ."

"It was quite a while ago we met too. How's Sabine? I hear great things of her."

"She's in Milan right now. Yes, she's doing well. She has two solo recitals in New York soon."

"Terrific. Maybe we ought to do something on her again. But for *Beautiful & Good* this time. I'm art director there now."

"Great!"

"Yes, it's okay."

"So how does it feel to be in full employment?"

"Oh, so-so. Of course there are days when I'd like the old lifestyle back. Taking time off when I liked, sleeping in late, drinking through the night, then back to work again—but times change, and I've had a daughter for two months now . . ."

"Oh yes?" Manuel beamed as if this was the most wonderful news he'd heard in weeks. You had to beam at new fathers or you could wave good-bye to that editorial job. If he could only remember the evening with this man . . . "Congratulations! What's she called?"

"Marie-Sophie."

"What a beautiful name!"

"You have a kid too, don't you?"

"Yes, Moritz. But he's sixteen." And a great guy, Manuel would have liked to add, but he shrank from saying so. For even he couldn't pretend that, since his son from his first marriage had moved in with them a year and a half ago because of his mother's severe depression, his relationship with Moritz had not steadily deteriorated. Full of hope for a father-and-son romance at first—they'd be kindred spirits, instinctive understanding between them, they'd watch football, go fishing, share bread and sausage—by now Manuel was glad of the rare occasions on which Moritz so much as greeted him when they met at breakfast. Where his son spent the rest of his time, what he did all day and often enough all night, who his friends were, whether he was going out with girls or indeed—God forbid—with boys, Manuel had no idea. And Moritz left him in no doubt that it was useless to expect him to answer these questions. Yet Manuel would only too happily have boasted of him: a high-flyer in school, the Johnny Depp type in appearance, witty, charming, incredibly self-confident. Manuel often wondered where his son got that calm, superior, composed style of his, that manner suggesting: I don't want anything from anyone, and if you want something from me you'll have to make an effort. It made people line up to court his favor. Of course, Manuel told himself, he inherits a lot of it from his father. The only problem was that he kept catching himself trying to get Moritz to like him, or at least not give him a condescending smile. And even if Moritz did show him a certain friendliness, if some third party came along Manuel couldn't shake off the feeling that he had only been tolerated just now. He had twice persuaded Moritz to have lunch with him at the Fôret Rieder, and it had been the same both times: Fanny and the waiters deluged Moritz with questions: how was he doing in school, what did he want to do later, how about an extra dessert, did he like the restaurant, he could come in on his own any time he liked, and on the second occasion Fanny even said that if he wanted to earn some pocket money he was welcome to work a couple of days a week at the Fôret Rieder. So far, so successful for Manuel too in principle, except for the incredulous glances that Fanny and the waiters kept casting him, as if they were waiting for some remark correcting what had been said about their family relationship. So to Manuel, Moritz was indeed a cause for pride, but also for a considerable amount of insecurity, and he preferred not to think about it.

"Sixteen! Right in the middle of puberty. You probably have a lively time at home."

"Hmhm." Manuel smiled and nodded. There was no lively time at home, none at all.

"Ah, well, I'm on my way to the men's room. Come over and join us for a moment when I'm back if you have time."

"Sure, why not? Except that I have to finish this report by three."

"The underground scene in Peking—sounds fascinating."

"You bet. It's all go there right now—London and New York are nothing to it."

"Well, come on over afterwards and tell us about it. Markus is sure to be interested."

"Markus?"

"Markus Bartels."

"Oh, *the* Markus."

"None other. See you soon, then."

For the next few minutes Manuel made himself concentrate on looking at his notes and scribbling something now and then. Soon he heard the door to the toilets open and close, and since August might stop by him again on the way back and perhaps cast a quick glance at those notes, Manuel wrote hastily: *In Peking "spring roll" is a synonym for someone who goes in for hard sex and leather fetishism. This caused Chu Lai to call his dark and sometimes truly terrifying spatial installation "Chambers of a Spring Roll Brain"* . . .

But August passed him by, and Manuel stopped writing. The notes he was really making were for a book project he had thought up for Sabine. It was to be called *In Bed With Sabine*, and it would be a kind of road photonovel. He was planning to go with her on her next tour and take some very private photographs, away from all the concerts and receptions. The famous pianist under the shower, at the hairdresser before her recital, watching TV after it, and so on. And a light, humorous text spiced up with all kinds of amusing anecdotes, giving the picture of a perfectly normal woman who ate cornflakes and was cross when she snagged her pantyhose. He envisaged the photographs as black and white, very grainy and very sensuous. For instance a large closeup of Sabine's mouth as she licked a cornflake off her thumb, or soaping her breasts in the bathtub—that kind of thing. Manuel felt quite sure, in principle, that his book would bring him success both in public and in private. The rave reviews had all been written already, at least in his head, and after his steady decline into the role of househusband Sabine would finally have to accept that he was good for more than just shopping, vacuuming, booking hotels, and doing an interview with her now and then. If only it hadn't been for Moritz. In a sudden confidential moment, he had told him about the project. At first Moritz seemed slightly uncertain, as if he wondered whether his father was joking, but then he laughed and said, "Just photograph the breasts and leave out the rest. Then it's sure to sell." Oh well, thought Manuel, he's only sixteen.

Around noon the restaurant filled up, the waiters were at work by now, and Manuel ordered a glass of champagne. He had hesitated momentarily, wondering if an espresso might make a better impression on the *Beautiful & Good* people. But in the first place he thought champagne at midday put a better finishing touch to the picture of a widely traveled and successful underground journalist, and in the second place he knew that without a little alcohol in his bloodstream he would be unable to go over to their table and sit down looking reasonably casual.

"Starting early again, are you?" said the barkeep, putting the glass down in front of Manuel with a skeptical glance.

Manuel was taken aback, and looked almost alarmed, but then quickly indicated his notes. "I have to get this finished in an hour—" he shrugged helplessly—"and you sometimes need a bit of fuel for that."

"Just so long as you don't start gabbling some kind of shit again and get the customers fighting . . ." The barkeep turned away.

Manuel resisted the urge to turn to the *Beautiful & Good* table at once, to see if they had witnessed this little scene. An underground journalist with a liking for exclusive alcoholic beverages was okay, being represented by the barkeep as a quarrelsome drunk was definitely not. And how could he explain to them that the barkeep was making far too much of an incident that could only be called at worst an unfortunate misunderstanding, so far as his, Manuel's, part in it was concerned? True, he had been slightly the worse for wear or he wouldn't have spoken to the man at all. But he, the man, had looked exactly like Uncle Holger, who was once his father's best friend. When Manuel was at elementary school Holger Fels, publisher of books on art and architecture, had gone in and out of their home almost daily. Then Manuel's father quarreled with him, and not until he was grown up did Manuel see Uncle Holger again, or rather his photograph in magazines and the arts section of newspapers, where he was described as the most successful publisher of illustrated books in Germany. And two weeks ago he suddenly thought he recognized him at the next table. Only the evening before, he'd had the idea for *In Bed With Sabine*. So what was more natural than for him to lean over and say, "Good heavens, Uncle Holger! What a surprise!" And when the man looked at him, baffled, "It's me, Manuel Reuter. Little Manuel. Don't you remember? You were always playing with me, playing at making books, and you said when I was grown up we'd make a real book together. Well, that's really funny, because only yesterday I—"

"I'm sorry, but you must be mixing me up with someone else."

"Mixing you up? Mixing Uncle Holger up with someone else? Listen: after my parents you were certainly the most important person in my childhood. Maybe even more important than my father. It was you gave me my love of books and photography. If you had any idea how much I owe you, Uncle Holger . . ."

"I'm sorry, my name is not Holger and I don't know you."

Manuel stopped short. "Not Holger?" And then some impulse ran away with him. "But of course you're Holger. Holger Fels. Don't you want to know me anymore?"

"Young man, you—"

"Is it an embarrassing subject? Because you were trying to have it off with my mother back then?"

From this point the situation rapidly became more complicated. Because now the man's young companion spoke up, in cutting tones: "Ludwig," he said, "who is this guy and what's he talking about?"

"No idea. I never saw him in my life before."

"Oh, that really is too much! Uncle Holger, think how often I came to your office after school and sat on your knee, and we looked at books together!"

"Looked at books together?" drawled the man's young companion. "So which were you after, the mother or the tiny tot?"

"Are you out of your mind too? Neither! And if I may ask you both to be so kind as to register the fact that my name is not Holger—"

"Oh-oh! When we first met you were calling yourself Dr. Zhivago."

"For God's sake! Keep your voice down!"

"Dr. Zhivago, did he say, Uncle Holger?"

"Bloody hell, my name is not Holger!"

By now all conversation had died down at the tables around them, so the man's young companion didn't even have to raise his voice for almost everyone in the restaurant to hear him. "But perhaps you call yourself Holger when you're doing it with little boys?" And in a singsong chant he continued, "Come along, little fellow, come sit on Uncle Holger's knee—yes, that's a knee there, just you take hold of it, little one . . ."

"Are you totally nuts?" The man who was not Uncle Holger leaned halfway over the table and punched his young companion in the face. Chaos ensued. The young man who had been hit screamed, first with pain, and then, when he saw his blood dripping on the white tablecloth, with fright; the man who was not Uncle Holger began wailing at the top of his voice and pleading for forgiveness; the guests sitting around jumped up from their chairs and made their way, pushing and shoving, to the bar; the waiters forged a path through the crowd in the opposite direction; and Fanny, who was standing by the tap at the bar and could see nothing because of her small stature, kept crying, "Mind their pistols! Mind their pistols!" in the belief that this was a gangsters' quarrel. Something similar had happened recently. Meanwhile Manuel sat comfortably on his chair with his legs crossed, sipping from his wineglass, and watching with interest as the man who was not Uncle Holger kept trying to mop up the blood on his young companion's face with a napkin. That earned him no thanks but blows in his own turn, and one of them, executed with a beringed hand, caught him on the cheek at such an unfortunate angle that he too began to bleed. At about this point two waiters reached the scene of the action, which by now, on account of the other guests standing around it, resembled a small circus ring, and uttering battle cries flung themselves between the supposed gangsters.

"Mind their pistols!"

There followed a general exchange of blows, deteriorating into a wrestling match, in which the crockery fell to the floor first, soon to be followed by the waiters with their respective opponents, and it was some time before it dawned on all concerned that their reactions were out of all proportion. The two spitting, scratching guests did not look like gangsters quick on the draw who must be overpowered before they staged a massacre in the Fôret Rieder, nor did it seem to the man who was not Uncle Holger and his companion that they had any good reason to bite the arms and crush the genitals of men who had been serving them soup not long ago. So hostilities gradually died down, the two pairs of combatants let go of each other, and soon all four were lying around the table panting for breath.

Manuel looked back and forth a couple of times from the men on the floor to the spectators still standing there motionless and perplexed, until finally, with a snap of his fingers, he turned to the company, index finger raised. "To drink or not to drink, that is the question. And which is nobler in the mind? I mean, those two were drinking only mineral water. So what I say," said Manuel, raising his glass, "what I say is, give peace a chance!"

It took a moment for his comments to sink into the minds of those present, but then Manuel came very close to being the next to lose blood. While those standing around greeted his remark not with the laughter he expected but with chilly outrage, the man who was not Holger suddenly sat up, pointed at Manuel and shouted, "All because of that stupid bastard!"

And the outrage very quickly turned to a lynch mob mood. The mere way Manuel sat there, legs still casually crossed, next to the bloodstained chaos of men, crockery, and chairs, negligently holding his wineglass as if he might start purring any moment with sheer well-being, was enough to make some of those present want to hit him. And to intensify this desire Manuel's remark, still clearly echoing around the room, was now followed up by his slur on the character of a man whom many had by now recognized as one of the outstanding German television directors of the day.

With all eyes turned to him, Manuel first began shifting back and forth on his chair slightly, with a helpless grin, then he suddenly stood up, put his glass down, assumed an expression of gravity, and bowed to the TV director. "I'm not letting anyone who has it off with little boys call *me* a bastard."

There, thought Manuel, that went home. And it did. The director picked up from the floor the first piece of cutlery to come to hand, and struggled to his feet. This time, however, the guests did not sit by inactive. Three men grabbed Manuel, three more the director, and while the latter was still trying to stab the former with a soup spoon they were both dragged out of the door and into the street. Meanwhile the director was shouting, "I'm Ludwig Braumeister and I'm not taking this sort of thing! You'll hear more about this! All of you!"

When their captors let go of them out in the street, and they faced each other for a moment breathless, undecided whether to attack one another, Manuel finally realized where he had heard the name, and asked, "Braumeister the director?"

"Why, you bastard?"

"Hm," said Manuel. "I'm sorry about what happened in there just now. It really wasn't intentional. But seeing that we're here—well, to make a long story short, for some time I've had this idea for a TV series . . ."

Manuel looked up from his notes. The barkeep had stopped in front of him and briefly traced a circle in the air over the papers with his finger. "Clear that away, will you? I need the bar counter. This isn't an office."

What in hell was eating him? For the benefit of the *Beautiful & Good* people, Manuel forced a smile as if the barkeep had cracked a joke. Slowly he pushed his papers together, slipped off the bar stool, and made for a free table with the busy look of a journalist who was an expert on the underground scene and never stopped work. When the waiter finally came over to him a quarter of an hour later, he ordered rocket salad, which he didn't like, and oysters, which he hated. But that, he thought, looked like a good power lunch for a man of the world. A bottle of wine with it—he wouldn't drink it all. Leaving half a bottle of Sancerre was surely about the most sophisticated impression he could give at a distance of ten meters (the *Beautiful & Good* people were sitting about that far away).

The waiter brought the wine, uncorked the bottle, poured a sip for Manuel to taste, and whispered to him, "Pull yourself together. The Minister of Culture's coming in later."

Manuel moved the wine around in his mouth, made chewing motions and slurping sounds, put his head back and let the Sancerre run down his throat, nodded at the bottle and glanced up, looking bored. "Who?"

"The Minister of Culture and his wife. And if you so much as make a peep you're out on your ear."

Manuel snorted dismissively. "The Minister of Culture—so what? I don't have time for that sort of thing." He pointed to his notes. "I have to get a report on the Peking underground art scene finished within the hour."

"Then that's okay. Just so long as you don't think of mixing him up with your uncle."

With my barber, more like, thought Manuel, seeing the minister in his mind's eye. "Very funny. And I also have a meeting just over there." He waited for the man to look briefly at the *Beautiful & Good* table before leafing through his notes and saying, without looking up, "So I'd really better eat something soon. What happened to my salad? Still sowing the rocket seed, are they?"

"Asshole," muttered the waiter, turning away.

Manuel watched him disappear into the kitchen. Well, that was telling him! What was the waiter's idea, treating him like the lowest of the low? As if he, of all people, didn't know how to act with such people. God knew how many Ministers of Culture he'd met at various receptions for Sabine. Usually deadly dull. Perverts, too. Always with actresses a hundred years younger than themselves on their arms, and still staring down every other décolleté. Although this one was married to a writer. A writer, was she? Although she did write books, and they were printed and presumably sold, so why did every cheap reviewer in the arts sections have to keep making snide remarks to the effect that she wasn't exactly

Proust? Pure envy. Because the arts section reviewer, sitting in a full-time employee's three square meters of cell, naturally imagined the Minister of Culture's wife being chauffeured about from one champagne party to the next, and whatever she babbled into her dictating machine in her five-star hotel in between parties, it was bound to be published as a book with her husband's help. What a mean trick! For of course the wife worked all the harder just because of her husband's position. He, Manuel, knew exactly what that was like! All those times he'd had to put up with people saying Oh, so you're Sabine's husband. As if he did those interviews with her while brushing his teeth. And what could people like him and the Minister's wife do about it? If they were to be taken seriously, they had to be twice as good at their jobs as anyone else—the immigrant workers of the culture trade, you might say . . .

Manuel poured himself more wine, registering in passing that the bottle was already half empty and his salad still hadn't arrived.

. . . So it was really a shame that he hadn't read anything written by the Minister of Culture's wife. But he wouldn't let that show. By the way, I'm a real fan of your books. (Novels? Philosophy? Interior decoration? The headlines and catty conclusions of those damning reviews didn't say.)—Oh, I'm so glad, I don't often get compliments like that because, you see, if you're married to the Minister of Culture you hardly get noticed at all as an independent artist.—You don't have to tell me: my wife is a pianist, I must say not entirely unknown, and I often have quite a struggle to be accepted as a journalist.—A journalist? How interesting, what do you write about?—Well, mainly underground subjects: the art scene in Peking, the Bronx in New York, Cape Town, Havana, Reutlingen.—Reutlingen?—Yes, Reutlingen, you might not think it but Reutlingen's a really tough place: drugs, hip-hop, spray art, the whole spectrum. (Do I tell her my father, a famous architect, once designed a comprehensive school for Reutlingen and I wrote a piece about it for the local paper? Simply as a kind of original counterpoint, suggesting that if you get caviar all day, every day, now and then an ordinary sandwich tastes great. And a bit of truth might improve the overall picture? Better wait and see.)—That sounds fascinating: Reutlingen: listen, why not come on to the Federal President's champagne reception with us later and you and I could continue this conversation?—Well, I'd really have liked to, but I did say I'd go and negotiate a contract with the people over there.—Oh, of course I wouldn't want to keep you from that.—Well, it's about a position on the editorial staff, and I'm not sure if that's really my cup of tears.—(She looks surprised.) You mean cup of tea, as the English say?—No, cup of tears, for don't you think every important decision brings tears in its wake? It means you're bound to be denying yourself something else which might be just as attractive.—(She begins to understand.) Oh, I see! (She laughs.) You say such delightfully . . . (she gets a kind of look in her eyes that says: oh, you could be dangerous!) . . . such delightfully unusual things.—Well, the underground scene doesn't stand for what's usual—in any respect. (I look her straight in the eye, with a Chinese spring roll sort of expression. She looks around briefly for her husband, he's talking to idiots of some kind about castles that need restoring, then she meets my gaze and very quickly runs her tongue over her lips.)—Think better of that editorial position, then, and come to the President's place with us . . . (She leans aside in her chair in a suggestive way.) . . . He has a big house.

A big house—Manuel grinned to himself. Wow, baby, let's go to the President's and try out his Louis Quatorze table!

When Manuel next looked around the room he had to narrow his eyes to get a clear picture. The *Beautiful & Good* people were still sitting by the window. He ought to make his way over there, slowly. But where was his lunch? And he'd finished the wine. He looked out for the waiter and signaled to him to bring another bottle. When the waiter was taking the cork out a little later, Manuel did not ask about his lunch. The idea of oysters turned his stomach.

"Hey, Manuel!"

"Hm?" Ponderously, Manuel turned his head. There was—what was his name again?

"Sorry, but we have to go now. If you're passing and you have time, look in at the editorial office some day."

"Hmhm."

"And then we'll do a nice article on Sabine. I've already mentioned it to Markus. So in principle that's all fixed. We'll

have to make sure the photos are right for *Beautiful & Good*—
I mean, they ought to be a bit unusual, sexy . . ."

The man was staring at him. Was that meant to be a
question?

"Hmhm, my idea exshactly—coarshe-grained . . ."

"What?"

"Coarshe, grainy photosh, cornflake onna thumb."

"Good heavens, Manuel!" The man slapped him on the
shoulder. "You're well tanked up, right? Probably comes of
your subject—the Peking underground!" The man laughed.
"What do they drink there, by the way?"

"Dishtilled dog."

He laughed again—"That's a good one!"—and clapped
him on the shoulder once more. "Well, see you soon, I hope.
Have fun."

And there went the contract for the editorial job. The
hell with it. A steady job? Not his style at all. He belonged
in the wild, no safety net, no false bottom to the box, nose in
the wind, finger on the pulse of time—a man of the underground! And that was just how he'd approach the Minister's
wife: My name is Reuter—Manuel Reuter—I'd like to work
on a kind of photonovel with you.—I'm sorry, but I have
a lunch date at present, perhaps you would contact my
agent.—Oh, agents, the hell with them, now listen: I imagine you standing on some squalid street corner in Brooklyn,
I see you wearing a bright red suspender belt, no knickers,
your lipstick is smeared, your knees are bleeding, and meanwhile you're reading poems by Hölderlin out loud, really

loud, until the whole of lousy Brooklyn and finally the whole lousy globe hears you, see what I mean, from the very top to the very bottom of society, Hölderlin as a lookout post on the world, and then you read Hölderlin's own damning reviews—did you know how often and how brutally reviewers tore him to shreds?—but that's not all, as a finale you read your own texts with *their* damning reviews, and at the same time you undress—naked before the world, do you understand, I am what I am, naked like all of us, naked like Hölderlin, and last of all we'll have a photo in which you look like an angel—now is that an idea I ought to take to some lazy slouch of an agent? Are we talking about art, sex, and eternity, or are we talking about clauses in a contract? Make up your mind, lady!

Although Manuel had begun devising this scene only in order to picture every conceivable reaction on the part of the Minister of Culture's wife, from a mild fainting fit to the spontaneous offer of oral sex, suddenly he could control himself no longer. He had to go to the men's room, urgently. Jerkily, he stood up and steered a course for its door with a firm tread. Who said he was "tanked up"? The fact that he then forgot that the door to the men's room in the Fôret Rieder opened outward, and collided with it violently, might look clumsy but was still dynamic. At least he wasn't one of those mineral-water-swilling wimps in regular jobs who couldn't manage to open a toilet door except with the help of a waiter or perhaps holding their girlfriend's hand. You often found them. Everyone knew it. Art director or whatever, but then: oh, darling, please help me with the door to the men's room.

The guests sitting near the door watched in surprise as the man who had just bumped into it stood there, swaying, and muttered to himself, shaking his head, "Cowardsh, weaklingsh!"

Finally he opened the door, went into the men's room and disappeared into one of the cubicles. There. Jacket on the hook, unroll the paper, sit down on the seat in three stages: there, belt undone, trousers carefully down, don't touch anywhere the gays have been, and now very slowly . . . oh, hell!

For a moment Manuel felt sure he'd be able to get up again at once. But then, in spite of the cold tiles against his buttocks and the coarse brush at the nape of his neck, he began to feel quite comfortable between the cubicle wall and the lavatory brush. And since the accident had happened, he might as well stay here a little longer. Have a bit of a rest before tackling the Minister of Culture's wife. If only the light wasn't so glaring. Just shut his eyes for a moment. And move the brush a little way. Mmmm . . .

When the fairy found Manuel snoring beside the lavatory bowl she would rather have come back later, but her timetable didn't allow it. She sent in a request to her boss for permission to materialize briefly, and soon after that she was shaking Manuel's shoulder. He opened his eyes, looked up first at the lavatory bowl, then at the fairy, made a pained face and cleared his throat: "What . . . what's going on?"

"I am a fairy and I've come to grant you a wish. But perhaps you ought to freshen up first. There's a washbasin out there."

"Aha . . . a fairy. A good fairy, I expect. Do I have alcohol poisoning?"

"I'm in no position to judge."

"I thought you were a nurse. Although . . ." Manuel raised his head from the lavatory brush, sat up with difficulty, and looked around him. "Although I don't expect they put you up like this in the hospital."

"Splash a little water on your face and you'll feel better straightaway."

"I'd rather have a shower. Anything sticking to me there?" Manuel turned the back of his head to the fairy.

"I can't see anything. But your hair is quite dark too anyway."

"Hm. Could well be there's nothing there. Because I mean—well, do *you* use the brush in a public lavatory?"

"When I still had to go to the lavatory, yes, I sometimes did."

"Then you're the exception. All those bastards out there—art directors, movie folk, ministers of culture—they dab their mouths with their napkins every ten seconds, but do they use the lavatory brush? Not likely!"

"Well, you can be thankful for that."

Manuel looked at the fairy with glazed and bloodshot eyes. "Don't you of all people start getting down-to-earth with me. A fairy! Let's see what you can do, then. I'd like four Alka-Seltzers and a glass of water."

"Is that your wish?"

"Didn't you just say I could have a wish?"

"Yes, but only one. And perhaps you ought to think again before using it up on four Alka-Seltzers."

"Ha! Then first of all I wish for ten wishes." Manuel grinned. This was all nonsense, of course, but he knew the oldest trick in the world to play on a fairy.

"That can't be done."

"There, you see? Let me tell you what I guess you are. I guess you're the cleaning lady, and you've come to work late in that transparent outfit, straight from some party, and now you're trying to be funny."

"You guess wrong."

"Very well, so you're a fairy." Manuel reached for the cistern behind the lavatory bowl and tried to haul himself up. "Can you help me?"

"No, I can't. I'm not a material being."

"Eh?" Manuel let go of the cistern and leaned heavily against the wall of the cubicle.

"Do you see that door?"

Manuel narrowed his eyes. "Yes. Even though you're standing in front of it . . ."

"Exactly, and it's bolted too. If I were a human being I wouldn't have got through it at all."

Manuel stared at the fairy for a moment, then rubbed his face with both hands and muttered to himself, "Shit, I'll never touch a drop again."

"Well, if you don't want to freshen up first I'll tell you the rules in here."

"Sure." Manuel made a dismissive gesture with his eyes closed. "Fairy rules."

"No, the rules for wishes. First, you have only one wish and you can't multiply it."

Manuel nodded.

"Second, wishes from the following areas are out: immortality, health, money, love. Exceptions are possible to a certain degree, but there must be good reasons for them." The fairy waited. "Hello?"

"Yes, yes, I'm still here."

"If you'd like to . . ."

"Oh, do stop all that about freshening up. Once I've freshened up I won't believe you anymore."

"Very well. But I don't have all evening."

"I bet you don't: if a fairy visits me it's only in passing."

"What?"

"Oh, never mind. Either this is just some trick or I'm crazy."

"It's not a trick, and as far as I can tell you're not crazy either. Just rather wretched."

Manuel opened his eyes and looked sadly at the fairy. "That's the word for it: wretched. I'm a miserable wretch, that's me."

The fairy suppressed a sigh. "I can see today is not your day."

"You can say that again. And you should just see what my other days are like."

"Perhaps you can think of a wish to help you change all that."

"Of course I can think of a wish." Manuel shrugged. "Nothing simpler: I want to *be* someone. Pathetic, isn't it? But who cares now anyway?"

"Could you put it a little more precisely?"

"Sure. For instance, I'd like to go back out into this stuck-up restaurant and have the boss and her arrogant staff welcome me as if I were one of those stupid orchestral conductors or editors in chief myself. I want to be highly thought of, understand? Maybe even popular if possible. If only someone would see what I can really do!"

Manuel broke off, rather alarmed. Talk about belly-aching—he really must be in a bad way.

"Right," replied the fairy. "Those are really several wishes, but I think I can see a way to grant them all."

"Oh yes? And how about throwing in four Alka-Seltzers too? Because otherwise I think I may not live until they're granted."

"I'll see what I can do."

Manuel woke in the men's room of the Fôret Rieder at six in the afternoon, and having struggled to his feet found a glass of water and four Alka-Seltzers on the lid of the lavatory. He felt too unwell to stop and wonder about that for long. Swaying on his feet and shivering, he tore the packet open, dropped the tablets into the water, waited for them to dissolve, and gulped the whole glassful down at once. Then he leaned against the door for a while, until he thought his sense of balance was good enough for him to make it out of the restaurant and find the nearest cab stand. But when he came through the men's room door and back into the restaurant, he faced an unexpected obstacle. Fanny and three waiters in their own clothes were leaning over a magazine on the bar and looked up in surprise. Oh God, thought Manuel, that's it with the Fôret Rieder. He'd be bawled out, thrown out, told never to darken its doors again. But curiously enough, the more clearly the picture of this debacle formed in his head, the friendlier their four faces became. Until finally Fanny cried, beaming, "Hey, Manuel! What a surprise!"

Manuel smiled, embarrassed. "Look, I'm sorry, I must—"

"Come over here a minute!" One of the waiters beckoned to him.

"But he knows," said another waiter.

"He hasn't seen it in black and white yet, though. It only came out today."

By now Manuel was looking at them rather suspiciously. Was this a particularly refined way of throwing someone out?

"Come on!"

As he crossed the ten meters to the bar, Manuel thought he might fall over any minute, and his head felt as if it were about to implode.

"Here!" Fanny put her arm around his shoulders and pointed to a story in the illustrated weekly magazine that had the highest circulation of any in Germany. There was a photograph of Moritz above the text. Manuel looked at the photo, then at the smiling faces around him, then back at the photo. He tried to read some of the text, but the words blurred before his eyes.

"Why didn't you ever tell us about it?"

"If that was my son—wow!"

"It's so touching, too! Here, listen . . ." One of the waiters drew the magazine toward him. "This is just the start, of course: Young prodigy, aged sixteen, passages from his novel to be serialized prior to publication in the fall, etc. But then . . ." The waiter turned pages and ran his finger along the lines. "Here we are: 'My father thinks I think he's weak. The fact is, I see him as one of those boastful small-time con men who talk big and can sometimes be very witty—the sort of character I've seen in old movies. In a way I feel he's living in the wrong period. When I was fourteen and went to live with him he insisted on taking me fishing, as if a fishing trip was some kind of Mark Twain Gold Award for father-and-son relationships. He'd never held a fishing rod in his life before, and I don't know if he actually realizes that it isn't fish fillets in tarragon sauce taking the bait but real fish, with eyes and twitching tails. We were once in a restaurant and he ordered a whole bream, he probably thought that would be impressive. The way he quickly covered its head with lettuce leaves was enough to show anyone that he was a man who'd rather eat his meat or fish without knowing where it came from. After that I wasn't surprised to see him cut the fish up like a piece of meat loaf, ignoring the bones. The funny thing is, I love my father for it. And I despise people who think themselves so much better and cleverer than he is, just because they know how to take a fish off the bone, and think themselves too good ever to combine all that with showing off a little—I mean, you've learned what you've learned and that's it. I was catching trout from the stream at my grandmother's place when I was five. Of course, he sometimes puts his foot right into it—both feet, even. Like when he brings out those pathetic sayings of his, hyping himself up, or when my stepmother's given a concert and he urges some big shot in the Berlin Philharmonic to give him the job of sole reporter for all the Phil's performances. But really I feel that's very touching, and I'm always delighted when something works out for him. I'm pleased when someone's genuinely impressed by his quotations from Goethe or some such rubbish, or goes along with what he wants, at least for the time being. Sometimes I think the reason he makes himself look so obviously ridiculous, and it's so easy to see through his tricks, is because he's a decent man at heart, and subconsciously he doesn't want to deprive anyone of the chance of recognizing it. He'd probably like someone to say, "Yes, sure, Goethe, very interesting—now, you just sit down and eat something, you've been on your feet all day getting the apartment ready for Sabine when she comes home, and repairing your son's bicycle for him, and . . ." ' ".

The waiter stopped short as Manuel's head sank to the bar counter. Fanny lifted it and pressed his tearstained face to her breast.

"Break out the champagne," she told one of the waiters.

A FRIEND

It was all the weather's fault, or I can tell you I'd never have taken the job. In fact the whole business seemed to me peculiar from the start, not to say perverse. But that morning . . . well, I guess I'd have stayed in the car even if a blind man had been driving it.

It was cold, there was drizzling rain, dense swaths of mist hung over the service station, and the field where I'd settled down the evening before had turned into a huge puddle overnight. When I woke around five my sleeping bag was drenched and my head was lying in the mud. I crawled out, wiped the dirt off my face and looked inside the jewelry case . . . I ought to tell you I'm a goldsmith, or something of that sort anyway. I'm sorry to say that laymen often make fun of me. I mean, it's true I never had training or anything like that, I don't work with gold, because my customers can't afford it, and whether "smith" is entirely the correct word either is a matter for small minds to debate—but I make jewelry, and after all that's the point. To be precise, I fit jewelry together. I'm sure you've seen paper clips, who hasn't? But did you ever think what enchanting earrings, necklaces, and bracelets can be made out of that inexpensive material? Of course if you have money you can buy diamonds, never mind how badly cut they are, or platinum—one of these days science will find out whether platinum causes cancer—but for people with lighter purses, people with the good taste and courage to choose something unusual, my creations are just the thing.

So I looked inside the jewelry case and tipped it on one side to let the water run out. Then I glanced back at the service station to see if any likely opportunities for a lift had turned up. I'd been traveling on business for seven months, and believe me, I'd had plenty of difficulty in getting from one place to the next, but this was the most impossible spot for hitching a lift I'd yet encountered. Just because of a neurotic couple who said I'd "stink out" their car, and jettisoned me at the first opportunity. But at that point it was only four in the afternoon, the sun was shining, and I was still full of hope. I stood at the exit holding my notice saying BERLIN for about three hours, and then I went to the fuel pumps and spoke directly to drivers. But no luck!

"We're not going to Berlin."

"We're coming off the expressway at the next exit."

"Friends are joining us in the next town."

"Sorry, I'm going the other way."—"But this is the only way you can go, it's an autobahn."—"Why, so it is! And I was thinking . . . dear me, I'll have to turn at the next junction. Thanks, anyway."

Well, you know how these things are, who doesn't? Around midnight I had some pea soup in the cafeteria and then went out to the field.

And now I had to start all over again, but this time in the rain! Sighing, I rolled up the sleeping bag, strapped it to my backpack, and trudged through the mud to the service station. I bought myself a chocolate bar and some chewing gum to sweeten my breath, and then I positioned myself near the fuel pumps, under the roof, and waited—waited, smiled, asked my question, said thanks all the same, went on waiting. By now I could just about understand how the drivers felt, because I was drenched, and when you're dripping wet like that it does intensify smells. Not that I stank, but I guess I smelled a bit musty.

The morning passed, it was midday, no one gave me a lift, and it was still raining. Then along came Retzmann.

He was a man on his way up in the world, you could tell from his car: not a mere means of getting around, not genuine luxury either, but a middle-of-the-range Japanese convertible. Topless when you wanted, but good value. (At the moment, of course, the roof was down.) The driver's door opened, and the first thing I saw was a polished leather shoe circling in the air above the wet concrete in search of somewhere to come down, which it finally did, landing at an awkward angle on a dry spot. The shoe was followed by a black outfit: trousers deliberately too baggy, a shirt cut like a jacket with a close-fitting collar buttoned up to the neck. Probably quite expensive, and it would be out of fashion within two months. The face above the collar was long and bony, with a large chin and small, quick-moving, knowing eyes. The man was around thirty and had a ridiculous haircut with a fringe—as if he wanted something soft and innocent to counter those eyes.

He picked his way past the puddles to the gasoline pump and reached fastidiously for the fuel hose. I approached him, smiling.

"Morning—are you by any chance going in the direction of Berlin?"

He raised his eyes from his tank and examined me first without any expression at all and then with revulsion.

"Why?"

No man of his age could fail to know why a guy like me at an autobahn service station would ask which way he was going. His "Why?" was mere quibbling, and made me optimistic: a lot of drivers will give you a lift just so they can show off in front of a total stranger. They feel that taking a hitchhiker on board is rather like going to the brothel.

I injected humility into my smile. "Because I thought then you might give me a ride."

He examined me for another moment, then said, looking back at the tank, "I don't like hitchhikers." It sounded as if he thought that a nonchalant kind of answer.

Aha, I thought, so he's that sort: dead set on being unusual, even if it's just unusually unfriendly.

I left my mouth open extra long, so that he could relish the effect of his remark, and finally replied enthusiastically, "Hey, I'm really impressed to hear you say it so openly! I mean, nobody likes hitchhikers, but how many will admit it? Not to my face, anyway. I genuinely think that's great! I really have to thank you—I learn something new yet again."

"Something new?" he asked, looking up from the tank, slightly unsure of himself now.

"Sure! Honesty, however brutal, shows more respect for your fellow men than dishonesty. Suppose you'd acted as if you'd be happy to give me a lift, and I'd got in and sat beside you, and after ten minutes at the latest I'd realized how uncomfortable you found the situation—well, do you think I'd have been happy myself?"

He looked at me, frowning, then hung the gasoline hose back on the pump, and as he wiped his hands on a paper towel he said, "Talkative guy, eh?"

"Only when I feel strongly about something. But you're right: I never use one word where two will do."

"Hm," he grunted. He turned away without saying any more and disappeared into the service station to pay.

I'd obviously miscalculated. He wasn't so vain that a few compliments would distract him from his principles after all. I returned to my backpack and put a piece of chewing gum in my mouth. The sky was getting darker and darker, and my thoughts slipped into the obsessive idea familiar to hitchhikers, that I'd never get a ride at all. I imagined myself trudging through woods and valleys to the nearest small town, where the last of my money would just about buy a ticket to Little Thingummy on the Whatsit, and I'd be begging people to help me send a telegram to a friend asking him to send me money . . .

"Hey. You there."

I looked up.

"Come on. I'll take you as far as Hildesheim."

Praise be to the God of hitchhikers! I snatched up my backpack and the jewelry box and hurried over to the Japanese convertible. On any other day I might have continued the game further. "Sure you've thought it over properly?" and "I really don't want to be a nuisance." But just now I saw nothing but the saving grace of the passenger seat.

"Put your things in the trunk. I don't want the back seat going moldy."

I nodded understandingly. "Great car you have here. What class!"

He drove the way such people drive: my car's the biggest prick between heaven and earth! He swerved into every gap that offered as well as a number that didn't, he hooted aside everyone driving at a kilometer an hour more slowly, he stepped on the gas like a lunatic, only to stand on the brakes next moment, and when he overtook he gave the other drivers a glance that said: oh, go jump in the lake! He seemed not to notice faster and larger cars. If one of those zoomed past us he was almost always busy just then wiping the surface of the speedometer, resetting the windshield wipers, or helping himself to a mint.

After conducting this silent autobahn warfare for some time, he suddenly asked, "Where are you from?"

"Frankfurt."

I really come from a small town near Darmstadt, but when I mention its name people don't know what to say or how to look. It's much more common than you might think to believe that everyone from a godforsaken hole like that must be a born fool.

"Unemployed?"

"Heavens, no! Is that the kind of impression I make?"

"Well, what kind of impression do *you* think you make?"

He was going rather too far, in my opinion. In addition, I wasn't standing in the rain now, I was sitting in a car, and that makes a lot of difference to your self-esteem. Not that I'd have let myself turn nasty; after all, there were over two hundred kilometers yet to go to Hildesheim, but I wasn't letting him get away with it entirely.

"Well, no idea, to be honest. I've never been particularly bothered about the impression I make. But I'm sure that's a mistake. I probably ought to be following the example of someone like you."

"Like me?" Irritated, he turned his head. "How do you mean, like me?"

That's the problem with wise guys; the moment they're personally affected you can forget about the "wise" bit.

Ignoring his question, I continued, as if it followed seamlessly on, "As it happens I'm a goldsmith."

He overtook a rusty Ford Taurus towing a trailer, and although history is not my strong point, I could swear he looked at the occupants with as much dislike as if a gas chamber would be just the thing to clean up the autobahn traffic.

"And you can't afford a rail ticket?"

"Well, you see, we all have to make decisions: Money or ideals? I've chosen ideals."

"Oh yes? You make red flags in your line of work?"

He laughed. A high-pitched bleating sound that seemed to originate of its own accord, outside the body.

I was happy to go along with him. "Now that's what I call an intelligent joke! It really is! There's nothing to beat education and a sense of humor . . ."

Even as I was speaking his laughter died away, and his hands angrily clutched the steering wheel. Glancing briefly to one side, he snapped, "Stop fawning on me and jabbering like that! And say *du* to me!"

I was surprised. There was a pause, and four luxury limos shot past us, which was his bad luck, because in this tense situation they were doubly conspicuous.

Finally I cleared my throat. "Sorry. If I'd known that you—I mean that you weren't like that . . ."

"Like what?"

"Well, like your car, like your suit, like your hairstyle—I mean, not an arrogant patronizing prig but a regular guy, the kind a person can talk too, someone who doesn't keep thinking he earns more than most people in his job and can do a lot of things better than most too . . ." I paused for a moment, and then, in a tone suggesting that what followed had been on the tip of my tongue for some time, I added, "For instance, driving a car. No, I'm not fawning now, I noticed it quite a while ago. I really don't know many who can steer a car so calmly through all the autobahn traffic, and with such sporting verve too . . ."

I cast him a quick glance to see if he'd swallow this. He seemed to bridle for a moment but then nodded, mollified. "As a matter of fact, you're not the first to say that. My mother thinks so too."

A very unbiased judgment, I'm sure, I thought, waiting to see whether he was going to mention anyone else as well. But obviously his mother was the only person who appreciated his driving skills. I did not reply, and looked out of the side window. A man of his age, talking to a stranger about his alleged abilities, who immediately cites his mother's opinion in evidence struck me as odd. "My friends," or "my colleagues," or even "my family"—fine, yes, but "my mother"? And without so much as a smile? I mean, who thinks of his mother first in such circumstances, and who'd take her opinion seriously?

As if he had read my thoughts, he asked, "Do you have friends?" And suddenly there was an undertone in his voice suggesting that he wanted to open up.

Surprised, I looked sideways at him. Had he decided to confide in me or something? Because I'd praised his driving?

Or was the other side of this knight of the road about to be revealed, the sniveling failure? Was he going to tell me he was lonely and all that . . . ? At heart I couldn't have cared less, but as you do when you've been considered dopey long enough and the balance suddenly seems to be shifting, I replied tartly, "Sure, who doesn't?" and looked at him with as much surprise as possible.

"Asshole," he promptly replied, catching me off balance for the first time, and I even began to like him a little.

"Well . . ." I conceded, "of course it all depends what you mean by friends. Real friends—I'd say I have three of them. And another two I'd like to be friends with, and one who'd like to be friends with me. The rest are acquaintances or people from my past."

I looked sideways at him, but as he saw it we'd obviously exhausted the subject. That was fine by me. My private life wasn't there just to while away the drive for him, nor was I keen to hear any confessions of his own.

We drove on in silence for the next twenty minutes. I leaned my head back and began to doze off . . .

"Want to earn three hundred marks?"

I opened my eyes. Had I been dreaming?

"What did you say?"

"I asked if you'd like to earn three hundred marks over the weekend. Plus board and lodging overnight."

I rubbed my face as if waking from a deep sleep, and rapidly wondered what could be behind all this. Three hundred marks over the weekend? Sounded like the good old days when the flea markets were still full of kids who thought that you got high on joss sticks and strips of tie-dyed sheet came from India. For Retzmann, three hundred marks must mean at most a tip. So either this was an idiot job, or he was mean—probably both.

I cleared my throat. "Well, I really had a date in Berlin tomorrow, on business, and . . . what sort of work is it, then?"

He took his time answering. Obviously he wasn't quite sure about his offer yet. He took his foot off the gas and fished a mint out of the tube. The mint clicked back and forth between his teeth.

Finally, without taking his eyes off the road, he said, "I want you to be my friend for two days."

I stared at him . . . . So that was it! Well, yes: his haircut with the fringe, his mother . . . I didn't mean my voice to turn fierce, but it did. "What's that supposed to mean?"

"What I said."

"Sorry, but you're barking up the wrong tree. It's girls I fancy."

Now it was his turn to sound fierce. "Nonsense! I mean an old college friend. A pal."

And then he began to explain to me, in brief sentences. His name was Marcel Retzmann, and he was a theatrical director in great demand. (Here he glanced briefly at me, and I made haste to say I'd immediately thought his face looked familiar, to which he nodded in a modest, matter-of-fact way, as if words uttered by me were beyond any shadow of doubt.)

After his schooldays, and his drama studies, he had directed show after show for many years, and these days he hardly knew how to cope with all the offers he received from well-known theater companies. There was just one problem: although he was very happy with this situation, because he loved his work more than anything in the world, questions from colleagues, his girlfriend, and his mother about his private life had been coming thick and fast recently.

As I just said, to some people picking up hitchhikers is like going to the brothel. This was the only reason I could think of why Retzmann, of all people, was suddenly telling someone like me his life story.

"Even at school my one aim was to get into the theater. I knew from the first it was my vocation to direct actors. While other kids were playing football, I was working in a market garden so that I could afford theater tickets in the evening. I read all the plays I could lay my hands on, and staged many of them at home in my room just for me—I was actor, director, and audience all in one. What I'm getting at is that even then I liked to go my own way, and although my mother was proud of my interest in the theater, which was unusual for my age, she worried because I seemed to be lonely. I never felt lonely myself, and there's still nothing any human being could give me that I don't get a hundred times better from my work."

He stopped talking to overtake three small Fiats packed to the roof with cardboard cartons and plastic bags. I wondered whether he believed what he was saying, and whether his workaholism had less to do with what people *could* give him than what they'd *like* to give him. But one thing was certain: Retzmann wouldn't leave his "friend" sleeping out of doors or feed him nothing but chocolate bars . . .

"So to avoid all the questions and irritating advice I got because I was a loner, even when I was young I invented friends of both sexes—naturally they all lived on the other side of town—I wrote myself letters, I came home at night drunk from parties I said I'd been to, I hung photos of total strangers over my bed. Later, when I was studying in Hanover, I talked at home about my new friends, and in Hanover I talked about my old friends at home. And that's how I've been managing until now. When I realize someone's starting to look down on me because he thinks I'm a workaholic with no private life, no fun, as they call it, I come straight back at him with a couple of anecdotes about nights on the booze and redhot affairs in another town. It's not that I'm ashamed of myself, but otherwise my colleagues might not respect me."

I watched him fish the next mint out of the roll. By now I was rather fascinated by his story—although mainly by the technicalities.

"So how does this go down with your girlfriend?"

"For a start, she's an actor, so she knows what she's got in me." He briefly wagged his forefinger back and forth. "She doesn't make snide remarks, but now and then of course she asks, all wrapped up in flatteringly solicitous tones, 'Wouldn't you like to relax for a change? Don't you miss your friends in Hanover? Why don't we throw a party . . . ?' Well, so this party—and she's not the only one, several colleagues of mine have kept on about it, it's as if in my position I owe the world a party—so this party takes place tomorrow. It's my thirtieth birthday, and everyone's invited."

I was beginning to understand. Retzmann fell silent and appeared to devote his mind entirely to overtaking two heavy trucks. I peered through the rainy windshield. There was a sign coming toward us: Hildesheim 30 kilometers.

"So how do you see it? I mean, am I supposed to run about saying hey, Marcel, remember that time back in Hanover when we blah blah blah . . . ?"

"Something like that, only you'd call me Retzmann, that sounds more like a friendship between real men. And then I introduce you as a likeable oddball who's always fooling around . . ."

Retzmann cast me a quick, sharp glance, and I grinned mischievously so that he could congratulate himself on being such a good observer. Meanwhile I was wondering how much more than three hundred marks I could make out of the arrangement.

"So you're not a goldsmith, let's say you're . . . how about you do some kind of manual job, but you've been writing a novel on the side for the last eight years? People will like that, they've heard of such cases. No one except me has read the novel yet. Of course I think it's fantastic, I've been urging you to finish it for ages. We'll drop a hint or so about its subject, no more, and then we'll grin at each other. As a manual job I suggest . . ." he looked down at me, "I suggest maybe you're a forestry worker. And in your oddball way you've come straight from work to meet me. Know anything about trees or animals?"

"Branches. Stags."

"Okay. We met when we were studying in Hanover and shared digs for a while. You can think up a few stories about that—I don't like garlic, I'm a light sleeper, money runs through my fingers like water."

I never had a chance to check the first two points, but where the money was concerned, his view of himself was phenomenally skewed.

"Well?" he asked.

"Well . . ." I murmured, nodding my head and taking my time. The money would be easily earned, no doubt about that. And the thought of the birthday supper made my mouth water. In this I assumed that the bit about money running through his fingers like water bore at least some approximate relation to the facts, and I pictured tables groaning under the weight of lobsters, roast meat, stuffed chickens.

Another sign announced: Hildesheim 5 km.

"To be honest, I wouldn't say three hundred marks was quite adequate for forty-eight hours of work."

"So what, in your opinion, *would* be adequate?"

"Hm . . . considering that I'm supposed to be telling stories about the way you throw money around, and we'd both be trying to make me sound credible. . . ." I looked sideways at him. We'd soon be in Hildesheim, and it was getting dark. I was pretty sure he wouldn't find anyone else to take the job, and I had an idea that for whatever reason, he thought I fitted the part.

"Six hundred," I said, and without taking his eyes off the road he said, "Okay," and I thought: Oh shit!

As I looked out of the window in annoyance, I felt his triumphant glance turned sideways on me.

"Don't kid yourself," he said. "I really wouldn't have gone much higher."

The pale gravel drive wound its way uphill past flower gardens, old trees, closely mown lawns, and a marble fountain, and reached a small castle. Retzmann parked the convertible right in front of the broad flight of steps leading up to the entrance hall, which was bathed in yellow light. There were no neon signs or notices to show that this was a hotel. You could have thought you were paying a private visit to the lord of the castle—or even, given a little imaginative leeway, that you were the lord of the castle yourself.

There were five comfortable leather armchairs near the reception desk, and a low table on which several brands of cigarettes and cigars stood, along with assorted bottles of whisky and cognac, and a dish of peeled walnuts. A fire hissed and crackled on the hearth in the corner, filling the room with the fragrance of burning conifer wood, and casting a flickering light on oil paintings of ripe fruit and vegetables depicted in mellow hues.

I have to say I was impressed.

The manager at reception wore comfortable corduroy trousers and a cardigan. He greeted us warmly, invited us to sit down in the armchairs, and poured whisky into three large, sturdy glasses. We drank to each other, and he and Retzmann discussed details of tomorrow's party. The guests would be arriving during the afternoon, and the first big drinks party would be before supper.

"I'm certainly not trying to persuade you either way, Herr Retzmann, but the menu could still be altered. Although I genuinely think serving cocktail sausages and potato salad is a very original idea."

"It all depends on the quality of the sausages and the potato salad," replied Retzmann curtly.

"Just as you say."

The manager lowered his gaze to his notepad.

When he gave us our room keys later he mentioned that the hotel restaurant was open until ten, and the game casserole was excellent today.

"Thanks," replied Retzmann, "but we've eaten already."

On the way to the car to fetch our baggage, I said, "Yes, sure we've eaten already: yesterday, and the day before yesterday, and last year too—not today, though."

"I brought some sandwiches, we can make ourselves comfortable in one of our rooms with those. Between you and me, the cooking here is nothing to write home about."

"It'll do fine for me if it's hot."

He shrugged. "No one's stopping you from going to the restaurant. But it's not exactly cheap."

"I see. Food is extra!"

"I told you, I brought sandwiches."

"And there I was, thinking people in show business liked to eat, drink, and be merry."

"Don't worry, you'll cover your costs."

"You bet! When I think of tomorrow's menu—that manager seemed beside himself with delight! How about the following anecdote from our student days? Just as soon as Marcel had paid off the installments on his convertible, bought his Japanese designer suit, and paid for a pair of handmade shoes, he blew his last two marks fifty on a bag of French fries! Did we ever have a feast!"

We had reached the car. Retzmann stopped beside the trunk, his small eyes examining me critically.

"I hope you realize you don't get the six hundred marks unless you do a good job?"

"So why do I have to tell stories about money running through your fingers like water?"

He looked at me in surprise. "Why, because it does." He pointed to the hotel. "How much do you think it costs to rent half this castle for the weekend?"

"Well, how much *does* it cost?"

"Okay!" He counted it off on his fingers: "One: sixteen en suite rooms for the night, at three to four hundred marks each. Two: our two en suite rooms for two nights, also at three hundred marks each. Three: supper, breakfast, and snacks in between, plus all the drinks, for twenty-eight people, amounting to around ten thousand marks in all. Four: shuttle service to pick up some of the guests from the rail station, sixty marks. Five: five is you. Six . . ."

When I was in my room, lying in a large, soft bed under a down quilt, looking past the wood carvings at the foot of the bed, past the gilded bedposts and out of the window, where rain was falling through the yellow lamplight, I wondered whether Retzmann, in the room next door, was glad he could afford two days of this Paradise. Or did the numbers go on swirling around in his head and keep him from sleeping? Was he stealing the hotel towels, or drinking from the minibar and filling up the little bottles with water, to fiddle the balance sheet in his favor?

I for one, feeling better fed than I'd expected after two ham sandwiches and an avocado, was on top of the world. I'd do my very best to be a credible friend for him tomorrow. In his absence, and given accommodation in this room, you could even actually like Retzmann a little bit.

Next morning sunlight was flooding the room. A pretty, big-bosomed chambermaid in a white apron brought me breakfast in bed and asked if I'd like any newspapers. I had her bring me several illustrated papers and asked if she was going to be at the party that evening. Yes, she said, she'd be waiting tables. Then she smiled at me and left the room. After breakfast I showered, put on the hotel's dressing gown, and smoked a cigarette on the balcony, looking out over meadows, flowers, fruit trees. Finally I dressed.

In the entrance hall I learned that Retzmann had gone out, and read a message he had left telling me to be ready at one o'clock. So I lay in a deck chair on the terrace and ordered a white wine spritzer. Was I intimidated by such unaccustomed luxury? Not in the least. I'm intimidated by a wet sleeping bag or an empty fridge, but if it was revealed tomorrow that I was Rockefeller's great-grandson I'd take it perfectly calmly.

I smoked my second cigarette, and the air smelled of lilac. Through half-closed eyes I watched the chambermaid putting up sun umbrellas. Would she like a pair of earrings?

Then I suddenly heard voices behind me. Or rather, one voice. "But Marcel, my dear boy! You can't say just champagne! You should have told the maître d'hôtel exactly what brand of champagne you wanted, or you're quite likely to find German sparkling wine on the tables instead. In Vienna or Paris," cried the woman, in a voice that could be clearly heard by anyone in the immediate vicinity, "in any of the other big cities where you direct plays, you can take it for granted that when you order champagne that's what you get, but this is Hildesheim!"

"Mama, please!"

"Now, now! You're not feeling embarrassed again, are you? Just because your mother gives you a piece of advice?

Really, Marcel, that's so silly! Here we are discussing your birthday supper, and you act like a little boy."

"Couldn't we leave this till later and—"

"And there I was hoping you'd finally straightened our relationship out in your head! Well, never mind that, I'm going to see the maître d' now and settle the question of the drinks."

"Wait a moment. Let me introduce my friend Archie first . . ."

I rose from the deck chair and went toward the pair of them, smiling. Retzmann's mother was in her late fifties, had a thin, bony face, two sharp lines of bad temper bracketing her mouth, and her silvery gray hair was cut severely short. Her bright eyes had a metallic look about them. She was wearing a long, dark woolen skirt and a large, home-knitted pullover with a brooch shaped like two birds billing and cooing. A bright silk scarf was draped around her shoulders, and a string of wooden beads hung from her sinewy neck.

Her handshake was hesitant. "So you studied with my son?"

"Yes, and we shared digs!" I dug Retzmann in the ribs with my elbow. "Hey, those were the days, Retzmann, you old rogue!"

His mother looked taken aback, and then made an effort to smile while she reluctantly looked me up and down. "How did you get your unusual name?"

"Oh, after Archie Shepp. My father was a great fan of his."

"How interesting." Her hand began fidgeting with the wooden beads. Maybe she really was worried that her son led a lonely life, but I had the impression that she didn't necessarily think friends were the right solution.

"My son tells me you write?"

"Well, yes. Just for my own pleasure."

"A novel, isn't that so?"

I nodded.

"May I ask what genre?" She smiled again, and once again her eyes gave the lie to her mouth.

I smiled back, giving her the full works, and tried to let suppressed pride seep into my voice as I replied, "Holy Scripture."

Her hand paused in its fidgeting with the beads. "I beg your pardon?"

"Well, I'm sure you know about the Bible, the Koran, the Talmud, all that stuff."

Her mouth opened, but no sound came out. Then she glanced briefly at her son, but he seemed to be intent on something or other on the far side of the garden. "Well, well," she said at last. "Aren't you aiming rather high?"

"Oh, I don't know. Anyway, the higher the cherries the sweeter they taste—or so they say."

"Hm." The lines of bad temper around her mouth deepened to ravines. "Well, I'll go and see about that champagne. We'll meet again later. Marcel, come and help me, please!"

Ten minutes later Retzmann was back beside my deck chair hissing, "What was all that nonsense? Who's going to believe a story like that? You can be a little crazy, fine, but I don't have any megalomaniacs for a friend!"

"So first, who *do* you have for a friend, then? And second, what else would take eight years to write?"

His lips narrowed to the vanishing point, and he stared at me the way he'd stared at the Fiat drivers on the autobahn.

I made a dismissive gesture. "Take it easy. I know what I'm doing. You wanted an original friend? There you are, then."

"My mother didn't think that was at all funny!"

"Is she religious?"

Retzmann bit back a quick retort, and then said, "She hasn't had an easy life. And as for you and me, another idiotic idea like that and our deal falls through."

When the first guests arrived Retzmann and I were sitting on the lawn under an apple tree while his mother freshened up in her room.

"Off we go!" I said, and we began laughing and clapping each other on the shoulder.

Seven figures like something out of a 1920s movie about the working classes came across the lawn. The men wore suits of coarse fabric with suspenders, black lace-up boots, and had slicked back their shoulder-length hair, the women were in dark wool costumes, tarty boots, old jewelry, and had their hair in braids. Only one stood out from the rest: a man of about forty in a greasy leather jacket, jeans slipping down, sneakers, and a T-shirt that looked like a well-used table napkin. His large, sad eyes held a constant look of slight surprise, and when he spoke the words came out in a rush, as if he were afraid he wouldn't be able to finish what he had to say, with the result that you could hardly understand any of it.

Retzmann welcomed and embraced them all, some with obvious respect, some with a subtle air of condescension. Then we moved to the hotel terrace, and Retzmann clapped his hands to summon the waitress.

"What a splendid castle!"

"Enchanting!"

"Marcel's a real crackerjack!"

The waitress came with champagne and glasses, popped the corks and poured the wine.

"What a treat!"

"And I always thought you knew nothing about drink apart from black coffee with aspirin!"

"A brand new experience: textbook bummer turns Epicurean!" said a man of around fifty wearing a tie with Mickey Mouse characters on it, looking around astutely. Retzmann laughed and raised his glass to the man with an extravagant gesture, as if this was the cleverest wisecrack he'd ever heard. Late into the night, when a young actress who'd had too much to drink tried the same witty remark on

Retzmann, she earned an icy glance and the comment, "I don't know that foreign loanwords are in your style, young bummer!"

Buses and cars arrived with other guests, and soon there was a cheerful company partying on the hotel terrace. Champagne and beer flowed, waitresses handed around little deep-fried pastries and cheese canapés, and a string quartet on a small platform erected specially for the purpose began playing classical music to accompany the party. Only two people did not seem to be enjoying themselves: the man in the leather jacket, who was sitting on his own in a Hollywood-style swing, firing off remarks to those who didn't make a wide detour around him in time and starting to read aloud to them from loose sheets of paper—and Retzmann. With every new consignment of guests he looked more hunted, his movements became nervous, and his smiling attentiveness to one and all froze visibly into a grimace. I watched him stopping the waitresses at the door to the terrace and checking that any champagne bottles they were taking away really were empty. He furiously returned a forgotten but still half full glass to a young production assistant who had more or less wangled himself an invitation to the party. Although this was Retzmann's birthday he seemed to be having anything but a good time.

By now my role was confined to just being there. I was Retzmann's friend from the past, and except for two actors who wanted to get sloshed with me because they were hoping to get parts from Retzmann that way, the guests contented themselves with meaningless smiles when they passed me. From time to time Retzmann came along and said, in tones audible to everyone, something like "How's tricks, old fellow?" And I would reply with remarks such as "Ah, the good old days!" and "Great!"

I was being gradually forced to the edge of the terrace by the groups and couples moving around, until suddenly I was right in front of the Hollywood swing, and it would clearly have been discourteous not to sit down beside the man in the leather jacket for a moment. He briefly greeted me, mistaken identity and all—he took me for some kind of distinguished figure in children's theater, and I didn't disillusion him—and then immediately embarked on some confused tale about cannibals that he had written as a play in verse. He began reading aloud to me.

"Just a short passage," he said.

For a short passage, it was a long one. Tipsy as I was, in the mood for quick jokes and a little light banter, I found his reading excruciating. I looked around for Retzmann to extricate me from this situation! Sure enough, Retzmann spotted me across the tops of heads and piled-up big hair, and made his way over to me.

"Archie!" he cried. "I was looking for you everywhere! Hi, Knut."

The grubby man stopped reading and looked sadly up from his papers.

"I can't come now unless you absolutely need me for

something about the supper," I was quick to say. "Otherwise I'd really like to hear a bit more of this . . ."

Retzmann didn't bat an eyelash. "Sorry, but the supper can't wait."

"Who's that?" I asked when we stopped at the far end of the terrace.

"Knut Schmidt, famous writer."

I looked surprised. "Sitting alone all the time?"

"Well, you found out what he's like. Wonderful on paper, but in the flesh . . ."

"The people here don't give me the impression they'd avoid a famous figure just because he's a dead bore."

"Famous, yes, but he can't give anyone a job."

"Is there really anyone here who . . ." I was beginning when a woman pushed in between us, flung her arms around Retzmann's neck and began chattering away to him, high on champagne. From behind she looked fourteen: red wool stockings, short skirt, dolly shoes, Pippi Longstocking braids. When she turned around to greet me just as exuberantly, without even knowing my name, I flinched at the sight of her wrinkled grandmotherly face.

"Lovely to meet you at last! Marcel's told me so much about you!"

I gave Retzmann an inquiring glance, and he gestured dismissively.

"See you later, Mareike," he said, giving the woman an unmistakable slap on the bottom. "That's another reason why I hired you," he added to me. "Since they don't know you, they all think we have so much to tell each other they'll leave me alone. Normally that old cow would have stuck to me like glue."

"What job is she after?"

"No idea. Probably wants to play Gretchen."

Retzmann took two glasses of champagne off a waiter's tray, clinked glasses with me, and we stood for a while in silence, sipping champagne and watching the party in full swing. And as we did so, something odd happened: I began to feel at ease in Retzmann's company. He might be an arrogant, conceited mama's boy who treated other people like dirt, but he wasn't stupid, and his dry way of dealing with certain situations impressed me. He understood things when it mattered. One glance had been enough for him to liberate me from the clutches of the loquacious Knut Schmidt without more ado. Contrary to what Retzmann probably thought of himself, he was a man of action, not the type for talking and thinking. I didn't want to know about his theatrical activities, he probably directed some kind of uptight, pretentious stuff, but I thought he'd be the perfect partner for clearing out a rich antique dealer's workshop, for instance, or palming off fake jewelry on him.

As Retzmann disapprovingly watched a couple disappear into the gardens with two bottles of champagne, I asked, "When does your girlfriend arrive?"

"She's been here for ages."

"Oh?"

All afternoon, I hadn't seen Retzmann in any exchange with a woman more intimate than the usual kissy-kissy-lovely-to-see-you stuff.

"Over there." Retzmann indicated several couples swaying back and forth to the string music near the stage.

"Which one?"

"In the red dress."

"Good heavens!"

I was genuinely shocked. Retzmann's girlfriend, whose "dress" just about covered her behind and her breasts, was dancing in the arms of the older man with the Mickey Mouse tie, and . . . well, necking with him. She had struck me earlier as a pretty girl with a nice figure who seemed to feel out of place here, in spite of her bold outfit. Even now, while she was carrying on outrageously, she looked as clumsy and awkward as a teenager.

"Why so surprised?" asked Retzmann.

"Well, if she was my girlfriend . . ."

"She loves me more than anything in the world."

There wasn't a trace of irony in his tone.

"Well . . . that's okay, then."

At supper I found myself at a large table with Old Mickey Mouse Tie, Retzmann's girlfriend, and Knut Schmidt again, along with all kinds of people with that classy proletarian look. Schmidt, who by now was very drunk, had given up reading his verse aloud and was telling jokes instead. His success with them showed this to be a good idea. It was true that his humor moved on the usual plane of rolling pins and stains of suspicious provenance, but it turned out that Schmidt could keep the suspense up, change tempo at the right moment, and deliver a good punch line. While the rest of the table regularly burst into laughter, Old Mickey Mouse kept whispering to Retzmann's girlfriend, who reacted with a more or less strained smile. Yes, she was pretty: a thin, soft face with dark eyes and full lips, framed in shoulder-length, tousled hair that made you want to run your hand through it. However, I found that I thought she was pretty only as long as I was actually looking at her. If I turned my eyes away I almost immediately forgot what she looked like, and when I finally managed to remember it was mainly because there were at least three other women at the party who looked very like Retzmann's girlfriend. Was it their hairstyles? Their makeup? The way they . . . ?

"So you're writing Holy Scripture?" someone suddenly shouted right across the table, silencing the other conversations and causing all eyes to turn to me. Expecting mocking irony, I calmly finished my mouthful and then wiped my mouth thoroughly on my napkin.

The inquirer was a good-looking young man whose wild thatch of short hair and three-day beard, plus the constant play of his jaw muscles, qualified him perfectly as the possessor of what people call a head of character. Except for his eyes, which were as dull and empty as if they never got to see much more of the world than their owner's reflection.

I replied, smiling: "Ah—so you've found out about my little secret." And glancing around, I added, "Yes, I do write a bit in my free time."

Then something that struck me as totally astonishing happened.

After a short pause, a woman said, "Holy Scripture, how very unusual!" And she laughed. But not at me, she was laughing in appreciation of my wonderful idea.

"That's really something else!" agreed another man. And a third, turning his back to Knut Schmidt: "Yes, we've had enough of all this piddling little New German stuff, a verse or so here, a short story there. What we need are great—yes, I'm right with you there—great and holy works!"

"Are you creating an entirely new religion, or do you see it more as a philosophical reworking of earlier ideas?"

Before I could make some vague reply a small, fat man cried excitedly, "Oh, come on! What does Holy Scripture have to do with religion? Let me just cite the names of Thomas Mann, Hermann Hesse, Proust!"

"Prost!" I said, raising my glass to the fat little man and nodding to him. I earned general laughter.

From that moment on I could say anything I liked. It was all regarded as "original." When I interrupted a discussion of the value of the Bible in the twenty-first century to ask the waiter for more mustard, my "earthy nature" was much admired, and when I replied to one question by saying I had no idea of the answer, the questioner nodded and said he wished he heard more plain speaking like that these days, instead of comments trying to shine where there wasn't any light. Even Old Mickey Mouse stopped pawing Retzmann's girlfriend for a while and made a few ironic remarks. Only Knut Schmidt was silent. He was tipping glass after glass of high-proof spirits down his throat without looking up from the table.

Meanwhile Retzmann's girlfriend was looking at me curiously. Once I glanced from her to Old Mickey Mouse and then looked back, straight into her eyes, with my brows raised inquiringly. She quickly looked away. What weird game were the three of them playing? By now, for whatever reason, I was getting so involved in my role as Retzmann's friend that the sight of the old man groping her infuriated me. When he next pawed Retzmann's girlfriend's shoulders I said in a loud voice, "Hey, you with the witty tie, what does a woman have to do to show she finds your attentions about as welcome as the men's room at the rail station?"

All of a sudden there was total silence at the table. Conversation even faltered at the neighboring tables too, and if the string quartet hadn't gone on playing briskly away, I guess the entire party would have witnessed the scene that followed.

Old Mickey Mouse sat there for a moment as if turned to stone. Then he loosened his tie, turned his little blue eyes on me, and said calmly, "That's the first sensible thing I've heard you say this evening. You can obviously express more than just a wish for food and booze. I'd like a word alone with you later, if you don't object. Ever written dialogue?"

Before I could even feel properly surprised, let alone get over my surprise, a pitiful sound rang out, a cross between a howl of rage and a cry of pain, and Knut Schmidt's fist, slamming down on the table at random, conveyed a helping of potato salad from his plate to his face. Through dripping yogurt dressing and chunks of yellow potato, he shouted, "After I've insulted you so often myself! In forthright or intelligent or humorous ways, in and out and roundabout, face to face, without any scruples—but you've never asked *me* to have a private conversation with you."

"Because you'd shit on the table just to show you don't think much of the sweet course. Artistically, you're practically in the next century in the matter of form, but as for content, you're digging around in old graves," replied Old Mickey Mouse calmly, as if this were perfectly normal table talk. No question about it, he was in control here—more so than Retzmann, and suddenly I understood.

Next moment the music stopped, and Knut Schmidt, who had half risen from his chair, fists clenched, stopped and looked around him in annoyance. A woman with white makeup and wearing a black suit came on the platform. For a moment Schmidt seemed to waver, wondering whether to make an almighty fuss. But finally he dropped back into his chair. He wiped some of the potato salad off his face with the sleeve of his leather jacket.

While the faces around our table gradually relaxed, the woman on stage said a few words introducing a little show in honor of the birthday boy. It began with a rhyming song about Retzmann, Retzmann, oh, what a clever man; then came a mime about Retzmann's productions, which were obviously rich in gestures; then a juggler who called himself Retzmann and gave the balls the names of various artistic managers of theatrical companies, and so on.

Knut Schmidt was now drinking spirits straight from the bottle, while Old Mickey Mouse was still working on Retzmann's girlfriend, but under the table. I looked around for Retzmann on the terrace. I'd have liked to tell him what a bastard I thought he was. The very fact that I felt like saying so, thus endangering my fee, was just further evidence that my attitude was no longer one hundred percent that of the hired help.

As the fourth or fifth number, Retzmann's mother came on stage. Up till then the program had not been exactly designed to arouse lively interest anywhere or at any time—let alone on a mild spring evening after copious glasses of sparkling wine and beer, and with a belly full of sausages and potato salad. The entertainment had trundled on while most of the audience's attention went to not falling off their chairs. As a kind of compromise they were keeping themselves awake with forced laughter. But now they suddenly stopped trying to find a comfortable sitting position and stifling their yawns. There was an intent silence. Did some kind of special reputation precede Retzmann's mother, or was it just her unique relationship to the evening's central figure?

With an arch smile, she smoothed out a scroll of paper in the illumination of the spotlight, bowed slightly, cleared her throat, and began in a solemn singsong:

> "Good evening, each and every guest!
> Oh, what a party! Quite the best!
> It moves a mother's tender heart,
> And she this tale will now impart . . ."

There wasn't a sound apart from the distant clatter of china in the kitchen. The suspense was increased, if anything, by the way Retzmann's mother's hands were trembling, while her upper lip kept sticking to her incisors and could be unstuck only if she pushed at it carefully with her tongue.

> "A lovely child who never cried,
> He was his mother's joy and pride.
> A charmed existence he would bear,
> Like angels' choirs free from care.
> But in the past and still today
> Men leave their homes and go away . . ."

Her nervous agitation was gradually dying down, and line by line her voice became firmer, the expression on her face prouder. All the same, I could hardly watch. You may know the feeling from TV talk shows where B-list celebrities bare their hearts to the world. The more intimate their revelations get, the more banal they are. You want to switch over to another channel but you still keep peering through your fingers, like watching a porn film:

> "The little boy was not yet three,
> His father left both him and me.
> His mother was left all alone,
> Without a penny to call her own.
> If only you could have a baby
> Without a man—with a fly, maybe?
> Flies live one summer, then they die,
> Leaving no one to weep and sigh."

Retzmann's mother looked around, and the audience laughed. Especially the men. Old Mickey Mouse most of all.

> "But though his mother might go short
> Her little prince must want for naught.
> No man should ever pass her doors—
> Those brutal beasts with their five paws!
> His mother lived just like a nun
> Though warm at heart and full of fun . . ."

I looked at the people sitting around. Were they as painfully embarrassed by this performance as I was? It looked as if most of them were amused, some even seemed to be touched.

The text went on in this vein. Mother and son on the high seas of life, now up, now down, now joy, now strife—I felt sorry for Retzmann. Was this why he'd disappeared? Had he guessed what sentimental gushings about him were going to be spilled out?

When the last line had died away there was applause, and my neighbor at the table, with whom I had hardly exchanged a word so far, leaned over to me and said, "Wonderful woman, eh?"

"Hm. Brutal beasts with their five paws? What does she think her son is? Some kind of miraculous virginal girl?"

I found Retzmann in the garden, sitting on a bench with a bottle of champagne on his lap. When he heard my footsteps he reluctantly turned his head.

"Old friend!" I wittily greeted him, dropping to the bench beside him. Although he didn't reply I did not feel that I was unwelcome.

I took a bottle of beer out of my jacket pocket and opened it with my lighter. The moon and stars were shining overhead. Retzmann stared across the pale lawn. He didn't seem to be sober anymore himself. Without looking at me, he asked, "Are they all laughing at me?"

"Far from it. They all want to congratulate you on your wonderful mother."

"Ha, ha!"

"They thought she was laughing at herself. Honestly they did."

"Bastards!"

Retzmann drank from the bottle and wiped his mouth. "I was watching you. You didn't look as if *you* wanted to congratulate me."

"Well . . . anyway, I think I could see why your mother is sensitive about the idea of Holy Scripture. She seems to be keen on immaculate conception."

Retzmann drew in his breath sharply. In doing so he avoided looking at me, as before. I lit a cigarette and leaned back. Champagne gurgled.

Suddenly he said viciously, "Well, they certainly know how to get at me now. I can see it already in rehearsals: 'Hey, Marcel, do you think I should make Hamlet more of an—er—Mommy's boy?' And I'll have to go along with it or I'll make myself ridiculous. They didn't know anything about me until today."

More gurgling.

"I had no idea it was coming. It was . . . ," and Retzmann spat out the words, "it was a surprise!"

The sound of classical music came from the terrace.

"Like sharks, they are! One little wound and they gather around you in shoals. Within a year I'll be the laughingstock of the canteen!"

"Well . . . other people have silly mothers too."

"But they don't recite lousy poems."

"She obviously didn't know it would upset you so much."

Looking up to the sky and following the progress of my cigarette smoke, I sensed Retzmann restraining himself. We sat there in silence for a while. When I turned my head, he was ceremoniously lighting a cigarillo. Casual as smoking may look, it's not at all casual when you're not in control of the necessary little movements. Altogether Retzmann suddenly seemed somehow . . . paltry. He had hunched his shoulders, his long legs were twined together, and his chin, normally thrust aggressively forward, was dropping in a stupid way. I had previously dismissed his over-baggy trousers as just a fashion mistake, but they now reminded me of vain little masculine tricks like concealed lifts in the shoes and shoulder pads.

He exhaled the smoke noisily. Then he looked at me for the first time, and his eyes had that slightly glazed, fixed look that either precedes some profound comment or is evidence of foolishness. Or both.

"I've always felt sorry for her. Alone in her apartment in Hildesheim with the TV set and her cat . . . do you understand?"

"Let me tell you something, Retzmann." I threw my cigarette away. "You're a piece of shit!" And while an expression of astonishment and horror spread over his face, as if in slow motion, I continued, "You're a pimp, getting in a blue funk because of your mother. It took me some time to catch on, but your girlfriend is getting jobs for you. And as far as I can see it's no fun for her."

He gaped at me. He slowly closed his mouth. His little

eyes began to swim with tears, and his lips closed in shame. Had I really struck such a sensitive spot, or was he much more intoxicated than I thought?

"I . . ." he began huskily, but instead of going on he raised the champagne bottle to his mouth. Then he said again, "I . . ." broke off and looked at the ground.

"Something wrong?"

Retzmann said nothing. Right, I thought. I got that off my chest, so let's crank the party mood up again! But as I was about to rise to my feet, Retzmann swung around and held me back by the arm.

"Wait!"

It was after some time, and what seemed to me much exaggerated swallowing and sighing, that Retzmann finally said, "I can explain."

But he couldn't—or at least not in any way that would have made me feel less repelled after the explanation.

Apparently it had been all his girlfriend Manuela's idea. After one of his recent premières, which was a flop, she'd asked what would cheer him up, and he had said, meaning it as a joke: directing a production for Old Mickey Mouse.

"He's artistic manager of the only big German theater where I've never had a production yet. He hates me because I'm more talented than he is."

Retzmann stated this as fact. Only a moment ago fighting back the tears, he was now getting into his stride again.

"And apart from being a randy old goat of course he'd be particularly pleased to take *my* girlfriend to bed. He's kept on pestering her at first-night parties and receptions, but like I said, Manuela loves me. She loves me so much she said, "Okay, if this production is really important to you, I can fix it." Holding his cigarillo between his splayed fingers, Retzmann drew on it. "And I ought to point out that I'm not a prude and I'm not jealous. Of course I was a little shocked at first, but after a while . . . I mean, if Manuela doesn't mind?"

He looked at me, raising his eyebrows inquiringly. I didn't reply. What could I have said? That *I* minded? Was I, of all people, to set myself up as a guardian of virtue? Obviously the rules were different in Retzmann's world, so what value would my opinion have? And anyway what, ultimately, did any of this have to do with me? Hadn't I been getting on quite well with Retzmann up to now, as a kind of extra in his production? We'd even had fun a couple of times. For instance, yesterday evening when we were eating sandwiches in front of the television and laughing at the guff the sports presenters talked. Or this afternoon, when we'd solemnly persuaded several actors that deep-fried pastries were good for the circulation of blood in the brain and kept you intellectually lively.

After a while I replied, "Well, if she doesn't mind . . . but like I said, that's not how it looked to me."

"Of course it's an unusual situation for her . . ."

An unusual situation? Oh, I thought, get lost! I stood up. "Okay, Retzmann, I'm going for another beer."

"You think I'm an asshole, don't you?"

I shrugged. "I'm the hired help. It's not for me to give an opinion."

"Hired help!" Retzmann jumped up. "Garbage! After a day like this! Don't you see how much I trust you? I wouldn't have talked like this to anyone else here!"

He had put a hand on my shoulder, and this was the first time I'd seen his expression so frank and genuine. We stood facing each other for a moment, and although I found the emotional aspect of the situation uncomfortable, I began to waver. Suppose Retzmann was the way he was, and did what he did, just because no one stopped him, because—how can I put it—because he didn't have any friends?

"Come on," I said, nodding in the direction of the castle, "it's your party. People will be wondering where you are."

When we came back to the terrace Knut Schmidt was sitting in the middle of a crowd sucking schnapps up his nose through a straw and gargling with it. He was even more successful with this trick than with telling jokes. Other guests had had a drop too much by now as well, a condition they expressed, depending on their characters, by either letting rip or beginning to babble quietly to each other.

Retzmann put his arm around my shoulders and propelled me over to the table where his girlfriend and Old Mickey Mouse were sitting.

"There you are at last!" cried Manuela. Old Mickey Mouse nodded to us with a wry smile.

"We were having a little chat about old times," replied Retzmann, pushing me down into a chair and kissing Manuela on the forehead. After glancing at the table, he said, "You don't have anything to drink," waved to one of the waiters, and ordered champagne for himself and the others and beer for me.

"Guess what Reimund just suggested!" said Manuela, obviously pleased to see us turn up. Unlike the rest of the party, she still seemed relatively sober. "He asked if we'd like to go to his farmhouse in Carinthia next weekend."

"Next weekend?" Retzmann had sat down and was fishing a cigarillo out of his jacket. "I don't think I have time then. I have to go to Hamburg. But if you'd like to go . . . ?"

He snapped his lighter and bent over the flame. The three of us looked at him.

"Speaking of time . . ." Old Mickey Mouse ran his tongue over his lips. "Marcel, I think it's about time we did a project together next season. I still have a production slot to fill in the main theater in spring . . . I mean, that's if your commitments allow it. I for one would be very happy."

Retzmann looked ahead of him, puffing smoke into the air, as if someone were trying to sell him china ornaments. Obviously his revelations in the garden had had their effect on me, because I suddenly thought I understood him, I felt somehow in league with him, almost an accomplice. I had difficulty keeping myself from laughing out loud at the performance he put on for Old Mickey Mouse. At the same time I didn't avoid looking at Manuela, but what I saw was a resigned, satisfied smile; she was enjoying the fruits of her labors.

"Naturally I'd be very glad, too," grunted Retzmann, past his cigarillo. "But I've already said yes to the people in Bochum for the spring. Of course it's only an oral agreement so far, but . . . well, Reimund, you know how it is. So though it would be a great honor—and I've really wanted to direct a production in your house, if only because it's not one of the really big ones, so you're not under so much pressure and you can be experimental now and then—well, you know what I mean . . . anyway, the fall would be much more convenient for me."

Retzmann's eyes sparkled above the tip of his cigarillo like the eyes of a poker player who has his opponent where he wants him. Meanwhile I was wondering why Old Mickey Mouse thought all this was necessary just to spend a weekend with Manuela. I mean, in his position—well, actresses, young production assistants, and other such girls aren't exactly a byword for fending off the advances of artistic managers. But obviously the pleasure of—how shall I put it?—cheating on Retzmann with Manuela mattered as much to Old Mickey Mouse as directing a production for Old Mickey Mouse, who hated him, mattered to Retzmann.

"Well, in that case . . . ," said Old Mickey Mouse, raising his glass, "in that case I'll have to shift some other production into a different slot."

"I wouldn't like to give you any trouble."

"No trouble at all, I'll be happy to."

Retzmann raised his own glass, and they drank to each other.

"To your production!"

"To us!"

After they had drunk we sat there for a moment in silence, all of us hiding behind our personal versions of an inscrutable smile, until Manuela suddenly asked the company, "Hey, have you heard this one? Why do dogs lick their own private parts so often?"

"Because they can," I said, and the situation relaxed in the general laughter. After that Retzmann told a joke, and then Old Mickey Mouse told one, and so on. As if a long anticipated duel had taken place, and everyone had been very excited about it, and now it had passed off without serious injury. We drank and laughed, complained of the people at the next table, played games with matchsticks and beer mats, avoided any serious subject, and it turned into a really fun evening, except for Old Mickey Mouse.

Around three the last guests came over to our table to thank Retzmann for inviting them to the party and have a last word with him before going to bed. Old Mickey Mouse, dead drunk, had gone off hours ago, with the forced grin of a man who has been defrauded. Because all through the evening Manuela had left no one in any doubt about whose girlfriend she was, in spite of any other arrangements. And Retzmann and I had worked together as a team, playing the game, making snide comments, tossing cues and ideas back and forth all the time. At some point we turned our attention to Old Mickey Mouse himself. "That's a really amusing tie you're wearing. Don't you agree, Retzmann?"

"Sure, very amusing! Wish I had one like that."

"You're not mature enough for it yet."

"You think there's some kind of connection between amusing ties and a man's experience of life?"

"Of course. A Mickey Mouse tie when you're thirty is childish, but when you're fifty it's, well, amusing. Anyway, a brightly colored tie wouldn't go with your hair color."

"You're right! I never noticed before, Reimund, but you're almost gray!"

"Suits him, though."

"Yes, suits him fine."

During the evening Old Mickey Mouse had become a kind of sandbag, and anyone at the table was free to swing a punch at him. Even Retzmann's mother, who joined us for a while—she didn't have much time, because since reciting her poem she had become the center of attention at the party—left no one in any doubt that she did not care for the stout man in the youthful clothes. At some point we had come to resemble the girls in a brothel who both need and despise their customers.

At three-thirty the terrace was empty except for the three of us and Knut Schmidt, who was lying in the Hollywood swing, snoring. The little platform had been dismantled, ashtrays and remains of food cleared away, and only a few bottles and glasses were left to remind us of the party that was now over. Two candles burned before us, and the dark garden lay peaceful and fragrant with lilac behind us.

As Retzmann went from table to table in search of any remaining champagne, Manuela said quietly, "I'm really glad Marcel has a friend like you."

She was drunk too by now. She put her hand on my arm, and her reddened eyes, small with weariness, had an affectionate look in them. "A friend who doesn't have anything to do with the theater and all that stuff. Know what I mean?"

I nodded.

"I haven't seen Marcel as cheerful as he is with you for ages. He's always so . . . so thoughtful, always wrapped up in his work, never has any fun. I think his work *is* his idea of fun, but otherwise . . ." She lowered her gaze. "You wouldn't believe all the things I've tried just to make him happy."

We sat in silence for a while, hearing Retzmann's footsteps and the clink of bottles behind us. Suddenly Manuela looked up. "Why has he never told me anything about you? Always just nonsense, stuff about friends of the old days, no names. If only I'd known about you . . . till today there was no one I could talk to about Marcel, I mean no one who knows him as well as you do."

"Well, we'll be seeing each other more often now, I guess."

"Oh yes!"

"Hey, what are you two whispering about?" Retzmann came back to the table and put three half-full bottles down on it.

"We were just saying Archie must come and visit us soon," said Manuela.

"Any time! Whenever business next brings him to Munich." Retzmann winked at me.

Then we clinked glasses, and drank, and told each other how good it felt to sit here alone at last on this mild night. It really did feel good, too. I was floating on a cloud of champagne and beer, and I took Retzmann and Manuela to my heart. They told me how they had first met, and I talked about a woman I love, though I won't get her.

Only when the sky was already light did we rise, hug and embrace each other.

"See you tomorrow, old fellow!"

"See you tomorrow, you old rogue!"

In bed under the quilt I was still thinking: funny how things sometimes turn out. And I fell asleep smiling.

I woke around midday. The sky had clouded over, and a light spring rain was pattering against the windows. Taking no notice of that, I got out of bed in the best of moods, despite my headache and dizziness, and tottered into the shower. As I dressed the headache almost disappeared. And a couple of glasses of champagne for breakfast would do wonders for the dizzy feeling!

I hurried downstairs to the ground floor and went into the breakfast room. But the tables had been cleared, and except for a cleaning lady mopping the floor there was no one there. I went to reception. The man who had welcomed us yesterday was sitting behind the desk, tapping something into a calculator.

"Good morning!" I said.

"Good morning." He gave me a friendly smile. "Did you sleep well?"

"Very well indeed! Is Marcel Retzmann up yet?"

"Herr Retzmann? Oh, he left two hours ago. Wait a minute . . ."

As he turned, chair and all, to a row of numbered lockers I felt a lump rise in my throat. I leaned against the reception desk.

"Here." He handed me an envelope. "For you."

I tore it open. My hands were trembling slightly, and the headache was suddenly on the way back too. There were six blue hundred-mark notes in the envelope, nothing else.

"Is that all?"

"Yes, I think so. Unless you had anything from the minibar, it's all been settled."

"No, I mean . . ."

"Shall I call you a taxi?"

"A taxi . . . ? Oh, I see. No, no." I put the envelope in my trouser pocket and leaned against the reception desk in silence. The man smiled at me again and went back to his calculator.

As I trudged down the castle drive a little later with my backpack and the jewelry case, the rain blowing in my face, I thought what a perfect production Retzmann's had been. So perfect that it irked me, for quite some time, to have had no opportunity of saying so to his face.

THE INNER MAN

Breakfast was an almost silent occasion, the same as every morning. Why his wife insisted on this daily proof that their marriage was on the rocks Jürgen Schröder-von Hagen had never understood. They had been married for four years, they had been sleeping in separate rooms for two years, and about a year ago, after Jürgen breakfasted at a Tschibo coffeehouse for a couple of days instead of sitting down on the dot of eight at the table laid out in the balcony room, Elisabeth had said, "If you can't even turn up for breakfast, I'm suing for divorce."

As usual when she spoke to him, her tone had been cool and controlled, and there was no doubt that she would carry out her threat, although she shrank from divorce more than he did. Her family, their reputation, and their name were all against it. She was a von Hagen, and all the von Hagens took their aristocratic descent as seriously as anyone could in the 1990s without being locked up in an institution. Divorce, as far as possible, was avoided. Yet it was an open secret to all Elisabeth's relations that her choice of a moderately talented student of Russian language and literature had turned out, as everyone expected, to be a fiasco. She had married Jürgen Schröder, against strong opposition, when she was still a law student, was rebelling against the lifestyle, sense of duty, and arrogance of the von Hagens, and wanted to live what she called a life of her own. Time passed, and after her wedding and the end of her studies—when she exchanged a world of lecture rooms and canteens for one of offices in old buildings adorned with stucco, and evening parties in penthouse roof gardens—she remembered her origins and learned to value the status that went with them. All that remained of the past was a husband who just didn't fit in with her new circle of acquaintances.

"My brother's coming to dinner this evening." Elisabeth's glance was still resting expressionlessly on her husband as she stirred sugar into her coffee and raised the cup to her mouth.

"Oh, is he?" said Jürgen, and corrected himself the next minute. "I mean, I see." For the fact that her brother was coming to dinner did not answer any question of his own, and in his years with Elisabeth he had learned, or had been obliged to learn, to choose his words precisely. She would set him right like a schoolboy even for small lapses.

"I was planning to work late today anyway," Jürgen tried to produce a conciliatory smile. If Elisabeth's brother was coming to dinner it meant that Jürgen had to make himself scarce. To the brother, a rich realtor and bronzed high society playboy, Jürgen was little more than some kind of vermin, and just as many children enjoy pulling the wings off flies he liked tormenting Jürgen in Elisabeth's presence (thereby, of course, tormenting his sister much more). He would ask about the health of "our little fortune-hunter," he wondered out loud whether you could support a family on a knowledge of Russian language and literature, and asked, alluding to Jürgen's attractive and rather pale appearance, how the family planning was going, didn't Jürgen have it in him to make babies, maybe women were only his second favorite sex?

Elisabeth lit a cigarette, puffed smoke, and watched him as he went to the window.

"Why are you such a wimp?"

Jürgen looked up in alarm. Normally Elisabeth was content with hints or a meaningful silence, and she seldom attacked him so directly, least of all at breakfast. Breakfast, she had told him at the very beginning of their relationship, was sacred to her as a moment of peace in preparation for the day, and while she was at the breakfast table she could cherish the illusion that eight hours of sleep had set the world to rights again.

"But Elisabeth . . . ! That's what we agreed. You said yourself, when your brother comes I'd better . . ."

"Yes, yes!" she interrupted, without looking away from the window. The sun was shining, and it looked as if it was going to be a warm spring day. She had noticed Jürgen at university because he looked like Montgomery Clift, and when she got to know him she was fascinated by his progress from village butcher's son to well-read student in a big city—

the idea that you could rise or fall from one social class to another still struck her as rather unusual at the time. In addition, the idea of going to bed with a butcher's son had held its charms for Elisabeth, just as Jürgen, even if he wouldn't admit it to himself, had never slept only with the woman he loved but always with a von Hagen too.

Jürgen stared at the plate in front of him. After a while he raised his head and asked, "Why don't we go to Prague for a few days again, like we used to?"

Elisabeth did not react.

"To talk things over. In peace and quiet. Get to know each other again. What with work and other commitments we never get to see one another anymore." He looked expectantly at her. Finally he brought himself to utter the sentences he had often prepared in his head in the silence of the last few months: "I may look like a wimp who can't do anything much, but what do you know about my thoughts and feelings and dreams? Don't they matter more than whether I'm soon going to take my university finals, or the way I behave to your great oaf of a brother? Of course I could insist on having dinner with the two of you and making sure we all spent a really uncomfortable evening, but what's the point? A man is more than his outside appearance in public. It's his inner man that makes him human. But it takes time to see and understand someone else's inner man."

During this speech of Jürgen's Elisabeth had moved only to stub out her cigarette in the ashtray. She went on looking out of the window, and nothing suggested that she had even been listening.

Jürgen carefully pushed his chair back from the table and rose to his feet.

"Think about it, anyway. As far as I'm concerned we could go next weekend." He stood there for a moment indecisively, and then added, smiling, "If we call the hotel in time, we might even get our old room with the view of the bridge again. Do you remember? Our swallows' nest."

On the way to the university Jürgen stopped off at the bank. He had his own account containing his own five hundred marks, more or less. It was true that Elisabeth paid for the food they shared, the car they shared, and the rent of the apartment, but he bought his own pens and his coffee in the canteen. That helped him to retain a sense of independence. If, even so, he had to ask Elisabeth for money, he insisted on *borrowing* it.

As he waited in line at the counter, he imagined walking arm in arm with Elisabeth through the Old Town of Prague, where they'd sit on park benches, talk and laugh with each other again, and in the evening he would reveal to her, in the restaurant, that his studies were taking so long only because he was writing a novel on the side. He had been working on it for three years, without a word to anyone. First intended just as a surprise, like a birthday song composed by himself for Elisabeth and a few friends, the novel had increasingly come to dominate Jürgen's life. By now he was convinced that with this novel he would not just make a triumphant comeback as Elisabeth's husband and mentor, he would also be acclaimed in the literary world.

"A novel!" Elisabeth would cry, just like in the old days when he'd told her that during his study year in Moscow he had played in a rock 'n' roll band.

"A rock 'n' roll band? In Moscow? Fantastic!"

At this time Elisabeth still wore flat shoes, knee-high socks, and checkered skirts, thus providing regular cause for mirth in the student canteen. Straight from her posh Swiss boarding school, she moved through the university like a perfumed innocent. If anyone drank a few beers in her presence she would wrinkle her brow as if she were mingling with drug addicts, and she spoke of hitchhiking with an expression that suggested it was some strange sexual perversion.

Jürgen, who had traveled widely with his backpack and whose experiences had been those of any young person who must get by on very little money, had seemed to her like a Messiah, introducing her to real life. Badly paid jobs, cheap lodgings, the basic food of a student commune—in Elisabeth's presence his everyday life was transformed into a kind of grubby heroic saga. Of course only just grubby enough not to scare Elisabeth off. Jürgen didn't drink and smoke, he spent most of his time poring over books or practicing his guitar, and his favorite way to spend a weekend had once been walking in the country.

Yes, once! How Elisabeth had admired his modest lifestyle! His lack of interest in material goods, his search for what was true and genuine in people, his rejection of all superficiality! And now? "Wimp!" What had happened to them?

The door to the street opened, and Jürgen registered a peculiar little man in a wig.

"Can I help you?" said the woman behind the counter. Jürgen stepped up and pushed his withdrawal slip over to her.

"How would you like the money?"

"In fifties, please."

Back then Elisabeth had loved him for himself, these days she wanted the kind of outward show cultivated by her legal friends. Yet she must know that he of all people utterly rejected pretense and false appearances of any kind whatsoever! He was himself! Or at least, he tried to be.

Soft light, a bottle of wine, their hands touching. *The fact is, I'm really writing a novel. I've almost finished it.—A novel? Why didn't you ever tell me?* And later, in their hotel room, he would give her the manuscript, and she'd read all night, and . . .

"Here you are." The woman behind the counter put the money down in front of him.

. . . And in the morning he'd wake up, and Elisabeth would be sitting by the window in the sunlight, and . . .

Suddenly a voice behind Jürgen's back said, "Hands up, no one move!"

Like everyone else in the bank, he gave a start of surprise. He slowly turned his head. The peculiar little man who had just come in was standing by the door brandishing a pistol.

"Everyone on the floor!" he demanded, but most of those present were too baffled by his appearance to obey at once. The character appearing as a bank robber in front of them wore a shiny black suit with a silk handkerchief in the breast pocket, pointed patent leather shoes with gold buckles, a wide tie with a pink and yellow pattern, and the suntan on his face obviously came out of a tube. His eyes were hidden behind enormous shades, the kind movie stars wore in the seventies, and the reddish brown locks of his wig hung down to his shoulders.

The little man shouted again, "Get down, and hurry up about it!" and jabbed the air in front of him with his pistol. Some of the bank customers were still looking incredulous, but finally even the last of them lay down on the floor.

The little man climbed over their legs to the counter and pushed a bag over to the woman behind it.

"I'm sorry," she said, trying to keep her voice steady, "but we can't get our hands on large sums in cash. There's a time lock in operation." And in almost pleading tones she added, "Surely you know that?"

"Time lock?" The little man wrinkled his brow. "What's that?"

"A mechanism to prevent more than a certain sum of money being paid out within an hour."

"So how much can be paid out, then?"

But before the woman could reply, the howl of police sirens was heard, and soon afterward car tires squealed on the street outside.

"Stupid cunt!" hissed the little man, and if some of those lying on the floor had been feeling almost sorry for the naïve bank robber, alarm immediately spread through them at the thought of what he might do if he panicked.

The woman behind the counter raised her arms defensively. "I didn't press the button!" It was true; one of her colleagues had set off the alarm.

The little man glanced quickly around him, then bent over Jürgen, the youngest customer in the bank, and held the pistol to his head.

"I don't suppose you can drive a car?"

On the instinctive assumption that this would rule him out as a hostage, Jürgen replied, "Oh yes, I can."

The little man snorted nastily. "Then you're just what I want, you fool!"

The negotiations with the police dragged on until evening. Gradually the little man let all the bank staff and customers go except for Jürgen. In return, food, drink, and cigarettes were brought to the bank, and a Mercedes with a full tank of fuel was left outside the door. So far the robber's demand for half a million in the trunk of the car had not been met.

Jürgen's feet were handcuffed to a table leg that was fixed in the floor. His back ached, and he kept shifting back and forth on his chair trying to find a more comfortable position. For the umpteenth time, he heard the little man say into the phone, "I'm not leaving without the money! And if I have to wait much longer I'll gun him down first and then myself, I couldn't care less!" The little man had taken his glasses off some time ago, and strong black hair showed where his wig had slipped. At regular intervals he took a small box out of his pocket and swallowed pills.

What with his fear and the breathing difficulty it caused him, Jürgen had been unable to think clearly for the first few hours after the police came on the scene. He concentrated entirely on regularly filling his lungs with air, and everything around him seemed to be happening as if behind blurred panes of glass. Then, when the danger of fainting seemed to be over, he tormented himself with self-reproaches for his stupidity in being fool enough to say yes when asked if he could drive a car. At the same time he was haunted by newspaper articles and television reports about hostage takers who cracked up. Ideas of death had troubled him and weighed on his mind since youth, although basically they had revolved around a great and distant event that was inevitably approaching him, but in daily life still remained improbable. Now, for the first time, someone had pointed a pistol at him, and the "great event" appeared before him as quickly and in as ordinary a light as a neighbor on the stairs. Not until it was beginning to get dark outside did he sometimes manage to suppress his fear. He tried to think of ways of escape, he followed the negotiations with the police, and he watched the little man. For some time now he had realized that the ridiculous old man's disguise hid someone young. The bank robber's movements were strong and supple, and where the makeup on his face was beginning to run, smooth skin with teenage acne showed.

The bank robber slammed the receiver down on the base. "Assholes!"

Jürgen quickly turned his eyes away. The bank robber swallowed more pills, then he went to the counter where cartons of sandwiches, chocolate, fruit juice, filter cigarettes, and champagne stood. He picked up a bottle of Moët & Chandon, twisted the wire muzzle off, took aim, and let the cork pop against an aerial photo of the Dresden Opera House. He sat down at the table next to Jürgen with the bottle and two paper cups.

"How are you doing?" he asked as he poured the champagne.

Jürgen looked up. What was he supposed to say in reply to that?

"Don't worry, anything's still possible!"

Very reassuring, thought Jürgen. Then the bank robber raised his champagne, obviously planning to clink paper cups with him. He couldn't be serious! And suddenly the fear and desperation that Jürgen had felt during the last few hours turned to furious hatred. What did this stupid bastard think he was doing? How could he sound so carefree and talk as if they were just sitting in a bar? And why was he looking at him, Jürgen, in such a weird way? Out of large, green, long-lashed eyes. Yes, those eyes. A couple of times since the bank robber took off his sunglasses, it had already occurred to Jürgen that such beautiful eyes were out of place in a coldblooded hostage-taker's ugly mug. And now the eyes—Jürgen couldn't make it out—were looking friendly, almost unsure of themselves . . . ? Did the robber think he was totally dumb?

Jürgen was tempted to give way to his impulse to strike away the cup held out to him and shout something, when he suddenly stopped. Yes, those eyes did look uncertain. And beads of sweat were standing out on the hairline above the made-up forehead.

"Go on!" the bank robber demanded. His voice was high-pitched, almost like a girl's. And that gruff manner hid . . . Jürgen was taken aback. Was it possible? Yes, of course it was! Now he clearly saw it all.

Jürgen slowly raised his cup to the bank robber.

"So what are you goggling at?"

Jürgen wondered: Would he be better off if he let his companion go on believing he hadn't seen through the disguise, or would the truth create some kind of link between them, making murder impossible? He looked at the pistol. It was in the bank robber's belt.

"Look, I guess we'll be sitting here together quite a while before they can bring themselves to put my money in that old car. If we talked about something it'd pass the time."

"*Your* money?" Jürgen couldn't help asking.

"Well, it's not yours, is it?"

Jürgen sighed silently. His discovery had given him such encouragement, and the rude answer had annoyed him so much, that without stopping to think he said, "It belongs to the taxpayers. Taxpayers both male and female! Which would include you if you had a job!" He felt very clever.

For a moment only the hum of the ceiling lamp could be heard. The bank robber narrowed her eyes.

"*What* would include me?" It was almost a whisper.

"Female taxpayers!" repeated Jürgen triumphantly, as if there were no handcuffs and pistol and he hadn't been taken hostage.

"Oh yeah?" cried the bank robber, and she jumped up, drew her pistol, leaned over the table, and pressed the barrel to Jürgen's forehead. There was no more uncertainty or warmth in her eyes now. "So what difference does it make? Is that any reason for you to tickle your balls all of a sudden? This thing shoots with a female finger on the trigger too, you know."

Jürgen was so scared that he wet his pants.

"What do you mean, you can't raise that much in cash at this time of day? Fucking nonsense! . . . Yeah, in hundreds and fifties, so what? . . . How do you mean, difficult? You listen to me, I'm not going along with this much longer! And the press will give you a rough time because the hostage I have here is a good-looking guy, and clever and brave, and the public will say, Oh God, why him? Just for a silly little half a million! . . . Shut your trap! I already told you I couldn't care less! I'd shoot myself twice over if I could! This is kind of my last party, it's going to decide whether I can carry on with the whole fucking thing anymore or not! . . . Did I ever talk my problems over with anyone? You got a screw loose, cop? . . . If you want to help me, then find that dough, and fast! Because I'm beginning to get drunk, and when I realize I'm falling asleep I'll end it all. . . . Two hours? If it's really two hours, okay. I can stick that out. But if you call back in two hours with more pointless chat that's it!"

The bank robber hung up and turned to Jürgen, who was sitting in his own urine and staring at the floor.

"Hear that? You're a real brave guy, you are!"

She had taken off her wig and wiped away the makeup. Acne and scabs encrusted with dried blood showed on her tired, gray face. But under its wrecked surface the face was soft, with the remains of baby fat, and though she might be acting the gangster, very ostentatiously too, she still had the eyes of a child: curious, innocent, sassy, sad. If you looked only at her eyes and her rare smile, she was almost beautiful. She couldn't be much more than eighteen.

She poured herself champagne, tore open a pack of cigarettes, lit one, and perched on the edge of the table in front of Jürgen. "Wow, do you ever stink!"

Jürgen raised his head. He had been crying; he was a pitiful sight. "Look, if I could just get to the washbasin . . ."

"And then attack me? Talk about a stupid question!"

"No, really! I swear I . . . I'm on your side from now on. I mean I really do drive well, and once you have your money I'll take you wherever you want to go." He broke off, and hesitated. "But look, first . . . I mean, I can't go around like this."

The bank robber looked at him thoughtfully. Then she emptied her paper cup in a single gulp, threw it away behind her, jumped down from the table, ground out her cigarette, drew her pistol, and undid Jürgen's handcuffs. In the staff toilets she leaned against the door and watched Jürgen undress.

"Nice ass you have."

"Er . . . thanks."

Jürgen didn't know which was stronger, his fear or his embarrassment. He stood at the basin, half naked, rinsing his trousers.

"You got a girlfriend?"

"Yes . . . well, I mean . . . not exactly. I'm married."

"But?"

"How do you mean, but?"

"Sounded like there was a but in it."

"Well . . ."

Jürgen turned off the water and wrung out his trousers. This was all he needed: a discussion of his marital problems with this crazy child! On the other hand he felt that if they talked, never mind what about, some of the menace would drain out of his situation.

When Jürgen was about to put his wet trousers on again, the bank robber said, "Are you crazy? Do you want to catch your death of cold?"

Soon after that, Jürgen was sitting handcuffed to the table leg again while his trousers dried on the radiator. He had wrapped a towel around his hips.

The bank robber was swallowing pills and peering out at the street through a crack in the roller blind. Blue lights were still driving around in circles, curious onlookers were standing behind the barrier, police officers were leaning against cars and smoking.

The bank robber had taken off her jacket, and Jürgen was trying to guess at the shape of her breasts through her crumpled man's shirt. Her body was small and strong, and like her face showed the remains of baby fat. Jürgen thought of the wink and the saucy, "Seems a shame, really!" with which she had thrown him the towel. By now he felt sure she was one of the street children who hung around the rail station, drinking schnapps and begging. Was she a hooker? The pills she kept swallowing certainly weren't for a cough, anyway, and they couldn't be cheap.

Jürgen adjusted his towel.

"Can I ask you something?"

The bank robber nodded without taking her eyes off the street. "Go ahead."

"You're still very young," he began, but immediately stopped and sought words that wouldn't make their age difference so clear.

"Was that the question?"

"I mean, at your age people don't go robbing banks." Saying this, he felt about eighty.

"Is there an age limit? Bank robberies only for those aged thirty and over?" She turned to him with a mocking smile. "So you don't get the dough till you're about to retire?"

"People of thirty aren't about to retire!"

Jürgen looked at the bank robber in annoyance. Why was she laughing? Had he sounded indignant? Because of that "thirty"?

"Well, the whole thing's ridiculous anyway. Of course you don't go robbing banks at *any* age, but if you do, at least not so young that you're ruining your life before it's even really begun."

The bank robber folded her hands, leaned forward, and smiled like the presenter of a TV quiz show waiting for a competitor to give the answer to the sixty-four-thousand-dollar question. "So when does your life really begin?"

She looked Jürgen in the eye, challenging and ironic. He avoided her gaze, as if words failed him in the face of such naïveté. In fact he did not feel in control of the conversation. He wanted to sound like a helpful friend, not some senior citizen lecturing her. She mustn't think of him as a stranger. He felt confused because she seemed to have so little hatred in her. He could have understood a rebellious young woman disillusioned by the world, but how did you approach a girl of eighteen who acted as if she didn't mind about anything but the money, who treated him like an agreeable but—apart from his role as hostage—insignificant acquaintance met on a park bench? . . . Well, perhaps not entirely insignificant.

"I don't really know either," said Jürgen. "But I think being able to choose what you want, and what you don't want is something to do with how much you've seen and understood."

The bank robber shrugged scornfully. "So what do you get to see with only five marks in your pocket? And what do you understand if you're searching the garbage for bottles with a return deposit on them?"

Jürgen almost burst out with his own story: how he himself was only a butcher's son, he'd had to make his own way. But some sense of shame kept him from arguing with a street child about who had the most underprivileged background. In passing, the idea flitted through his head that seen in this light, his marriage to Elisabeth was perhaps not entirely unlike a bank raid.

"Do you really think you'll bring this robbery off? Because if you don't, five marks in your pocket and the freedom to go where you please are wonderful by comparison."

"Wonderful!" The bank robber laughed out loud.

"Well, have it your own way. But I've had it that wonderful way for some time, and like I said, if I don't get the money, the hell with any 'by comparison.'"

"You don't mean that seriously!" Jürgen sat upright in his chair, as well as he could with a towel around his hips and his feet fettered, and said earnestly, "Not the way you talk and laugh, the way you enjoy the champagne, the trouble you took over your disguise! That's not how someone who wants to die acts!"

The bank robber looked at him for a moment in surprise, then shook her head as if banishing thoughts of some kind, and suddenly grinned. "Not a bad disguise, okay? I nicked it from an old queen who was after Benny."

Jürgen waited to see if she was going to say any more, but the bank robber turned away, went to the counter, and opened another pack of cigarettes. She smoked at most two or three out of every pack, and the front room of the bank had open and almost-full packs of Winstons lying around everywhere.

After a while Jürgen asked, "Who's Benny?" hoping that if he went carefully enough now he might get the girl's façade of indifference to crumble. But she didn't answer. Jürgen looked at the back of her head, which was turned toward him, and the smoke rising in the air above it. Had the old queen been *after Benny* because the bank robber herself wasn't anymore, or because Benny wasn't after her anymore? Her great love? Perhaps she wasn't looking for money after all, but death?

Jürgen took a gulp from the cardboard cup, then another, emptied it and poured himself more champagne. Suddenly he found he was imagining himself in bed in the Prague hotel with the bank robber instead of Elisabeth. Confused, he upset the cup, and champagne spilled over his legs.

"You know what a good hostage-taking story would be?"

Jürgen looked up from his attempt to mop away the sticky liquid with the towel without exposing his butt.

"No. What?"

The bank robber turned around. "If the hostage went along with it. If the hostage wanted out too. Get it? Then the hostage taker wouldn't have to watch the hostage any more, they'd be in it together. The cops would go on thinking it was for real and let them both go. And of course they'd share the money."

It took Jürgen a moment to understand. Then he stared at her, astonished. Was she trying to fool him? Or had he really managed to win her trust? If so, now what? For God's sake! Now she was smiling. Jürgen wasn't used to drink, and the champagne went straight to his head. Under the bank robber's gaze he turned red, and quickly looked down at the floor.

He cleared his throat. His voice husky, he asked, "So where are you planning to go?"

"Somewhere in the sun." Then she looked at him thoughtfully for a moment, before slyly winking. "You're thinking you can pretend to me, right?"

Jürgen looked up and shook his head. "No, really I'm not! It's just so . . . confusing."

They were facing each other across the table, empty champagne bottles and countless opened cigarette packs between them. There was still an hour to go before the deadline agreed with the police for finally handing over the half million.

The bank robber, tipping her chair backward, had clasped her hands behind her head and her eyes were glazed and bloodshot. She had been on her feet for over forty-eight hours, and when she sensed that, in some strange way, Jürgen liked her and would probably not try to prevent her flight, her tension relaxed, and she had fallen into a state of exhaustion from which neither champagne nor pills could arouse her.

Jürgen, on the contrary, was wide awake and in a state of intoxication: ideas and questions piled into his mind, vague images of happiness and adventure rose before his eyes. He hadn't done anything wrong yet, but . . . suppose he really did go along with her? While she was threatening him with the pistol there was nothing else he could do anyway, but what if she took her eyes off him for a moment? Had he just gone crazy in these last few hours of humiliation and fear, or had the girl, with her ideas of staking everything on a single card and running her head against the wall, touched a chord in him that he had thought was silenced forever? His bold move in flinging the inheritance of the butcher shop back in his father's face, the rage with which he had fled the parental home and hitchhiked to the big city without a penny in his pocket, the courage that had never left him in Moscow even as a student who hardly went out, had few contacts, and was rhythm guitarist in a third-rate weekend band . . . No, he really hadn't always been a wimp who turned up for breakfast at eight in the morning on his wife's whim! Could his involvement in the bank raid be a sign from Fate? Had he, perhaps, just been waiting for something like this? And didn't the bank robber's eyes and her smile radiate more life than anything he'd known these last few years . . . ?

"Tell me about your wife."

Jürgen looked up. "There's not much to tell." He poured more wine. His cheeks were glowing. He was enjoying the champagne more and more. "She's an attorney. We hardly ever see each other. And when we do we have nothing to say."

Was the bank robber beautiful? Jürgen smiled to himself. What did beauty have to do with it?

"And how about you?" asked the bank robber, keen to keep the conversation and her circulation going.

"What do you mean, me?"

"What do you do?"

He hesitated. "I'm studying." Then he took a deep breath and announced, "But really I'm writing a novel."

"A novel?" The bank robber perked up, and for a moment her eyes were almost clear. "Wow, terrific!"

Jürgen stopped short, and then goose bumps came over him.

"I used to write stuff too, just short things, kind of a diary. And I read like crazy . . . Well, I did till I left home. Books cost. What's yours about?"

Jürgen felt like laughing out loud. Here he was, tormenting himself only a moment ago with the fear of death, and now he was sitting drinking champagne with the bank robber, feeling that he could lose himself in her green eyes, and on the point of talking, for the first time, about his novel. The novel he'd written for Elisabeth . . . . Grinning broadly inside himself, he thought: She can get her legal friends to read her their ideas for new laws!

The merriment suddenly emanating from Jürgen made the bank robber stop short. She tipped her chair forward again, leaned toward him, and asked, "You think it's so funny for someone like me to have read books?"

Jürgen took fright at her icy tone. He swiftly said, "Oh no! Not at all! It's just . . . I mean, I never told anyone about my novel before, and doing it now, in this situation . . ."

They sat there for a moment in silence. Then the bank robber took a cigarette, sat back in her chair, and said, "Bet you I read more in the past than you did. I had a real passion for it. For reading anything, even just the back of a cornflakes box. I was always reading in school too, under the desk, out in the yard. Until they went and took the books away from me."

"Who did?"

"My parents, the teachers, whoever. I told you, I was addicted. Didn't take in anything else. I liked fairy tales best, or something funny."

"Hm." Jürgen raised his shoulders, smiling. "I'm sorry to say what I write isn't either funny or a fairy tale."

"Why are you sorry?"

"What do you mean, why?"

"Well, you chose what to write about."

"Oh, I see. I meant . . . sorry for not giving a woman like you what she likes best. And then . . ." Jürgen took another gulp of champagne. He himself couldn't have said if he really took the bank robber seriously in this conversation, or if he just wanted to. But "want to" he certainly did! His life, the novel, love, his future—the room was suddenly full of great subjects, and doubts of the person he was talking to were inappropriate. "And then, I don't really choose what and how I write."

"So?"

"So a story just comes to me—I've no idea why it's that story and not another—and then I try to tell it in my own way as well as I can."

The bank robber was getting impatient. "What's your novel about, then?"

"Hm, well, what's it about . . . ?" Jürgen laughed in an artificial way. "I can't really put that in two or three sentences . . ."

He fell silent. The bank robber watched him compressing his lips, obviously trying to find something to say. She waited for him to go on, and then suddenly snapped angrily, "Then put it in ten!" And drew her pistol. "In case it hasn't dawned on you, I'm just about done in! So tell me something to keep me awake!"

Jürgen had jumped, and now shrank back into his chair in alarm. "Yes, sure!" And as he looked back and forth from the gun to the bank robber's eyes he added: "Please . . . !"

The bank robber kept the pistol aimed at Jürgen for a moment, then let it drop on the table with a scornful look and sank back in her own chair, exhausted. "Go on, then!"

Jürgen slowly let his shoulders slump and folded his trembling hands in his lap. Everything could change so quickly! He tried to concentrate.

Hesitantly, he began, "Well, it's about this man in a village who's inherited a lot of money and doesn't have to work."

"A fairy tale after all." The bank robber grinned faintly.

"Maybe. I don't know." Jürgen desperately sought the main strand of the story, the one that he could put into words, picking it out of the different confused levels of the novel and the many narrative viewpoints. If he'd only known the circumstances in which he'd have to summarize his story for the first time, and what depended on it . . . . He would have liked to tell a story from the Brothers Grimm, but he was afraid that, well read as the bank robber claimed to be, she might notice and lose her temper again.

"Well, anyway, the whole village is making snide remarks about him, they say he's lazy and soft and he'll never get anywhere in life. And as he doesn't have a wife or children, a lot of people also say he's gay. In fact he's kind of like the village idiot. It starts in the morning with the postman grinning at him and shouting that he's afraid there's nothing for him today, because apart from bills and junk mail nothing ever does come for him . . ."

Jürgen's narrative slowly gathered speed. Without looking at the bank robber, concentrating his fixed gaze at the floor, he described, scene by scene, the humiliations suffered by his protagonist for the first sixty pages. Inflicted on him by the neighbors, the village mayor, the butcher, the children in the street. And from one humiliation to the next he became more and more sure of himself. Soon he actually thought that the exhaustive way he had described this part of the action, to which he had clung at first only out of fear, was necessary to make the extent of the following conflict comprehensible. Less and less of a hostage, more and more of a writer, he spurred himself on: I'll do it, he thought, she's going to think it's exciting!

Meanwhile the bank robber put her legs up on the table and crossed her arms below her breasts. Her head sank slowly to her shoulder. She kept her eyes open, but the pupils slipped sideways, and she seemed to be squinting.

". . . So one day he decides to catch a train every morning as if he were going to work. He comes back in the evening, and in the village inn, with the farmers and tradesmen, he acts as if his working day had exhausted him and he just wants a couple of beers before bedtime. But in fact it's at night that he really begins to work . . ."

Jürgen stopped, and glanced aside for the first time since he had begun telling his story. At the sight of the body slumped unconscious in the chair he started, and his forehead, flushed with enthusiasm and champagne, furrowed. He was hardly afraid at all anymore, or at least not for his life. The bank robber, disturbed by the sudden silence, moved her head and murmured, "Go on!"

Jürgen nodded. The climax of his novel was just coming. Out loud, and in as penetrating a voice as possible, he went on, "He writes a book about the village, and how shabbily it treats him simply because he doesn't fit in with what the villagers are used to. Of course he'd like the book to make him famous, just to show everyone . . ."

Now Jürgen told the story of the book within the book. His idea, he explained, had been to write something that worked like those nesting Russian dolls, each containing the same doll again when you open it, only smaller.

The bank robber had closed her eyes. By now she was tired of the sound of Jürgen's voice, but she no longer had the strength to do anything about it. Pictures were going around in her head: pictures of banknotes, palm-fringed beaches, policemen, Benny's funeral. They went around faster and faster until they carried her away with them. She wanted to call for help, but not a sound came out.

". . . But one night there's a fire in the house next door, and being the only person in the village still awake he manages to save two children who would have burned to death in their beds but for him. So the next day he's suddenly a hero. The newspaper writes about him, the TV people come, the children's parents keep on thanking him, and everyone drinks to him in the bar in the evening. Everything about him that they despised before is suddenly good, and he's accepted as a man who can rise to an extraordinary occasion. Meanwhile his book, criticizing everyone in the village, is almost finished . . ."

Jürgen fell silent. The bank robber had begun breathing deeply and regularly. At first he felt confused, then furious. He felt like waking her to say, "Look, the good bit is just coming! The crucial question, the heart of the novel!" He'd been preparing for it all this time, and now, just as he was about to launch into it . . .

For a while he did not move. Then he poured himself more champagne, as quietly as possible, and emptied the paper cup in a single draft. His eye fell on the pistol.

Ten minutes later Jürgen was still staring at the black, gleaming metal. He had never held a gun before. He slowly realized that he was free now, safe. Safe? He felt stunned, numb, rejected, somehow fallen from grace, worthless. He had so often imagined what it would be like appearing before the public with his story for the first time. It wasn't his fault that it happened during a bank robbery and he only had to say what had happened in the robbery. He'd been waiting three years for this moment. *But I'm really writing a novel . . .* He looked up and saw the bank robber's face. Saliva was dribbling from the corner of her mouth.

Jürgen's eyes roamed over the room. Cigarette packs, empty bottles, fallen chairs, garbage. The poster with the aerial view of the Dresden Opera House was torn where the champagne cork had hit it. The ceiling lamps bathed everything in pallid light. He heard them humming, and for the first time, he thought, he heard noises outside. The distant sound of engines, doors slamming. His glance fell on his trousers draped over the radiator. As if in a reflex reaction he closed his eyes, and shook his head. What had he thought all this was? A romantic adventure complete with literary discussion? The beginning of a new and better life?

Without putting the pistol down, he poured more champagne and raised the cup to his lips. He felt as if he were drinking water. Alcohol seemed to have no effect on him anymore.

Was his life really so wretched that it took only a single day and a girl to question it, to put it all out of joint?

He looked at the pistol again. If the bank robber's finger had twitched too nervously just for a moment, he'd have been dead. What were the emotions and ideas that arose in such a situation worth? Yet all the same, how euphoric he had felt, how—well, happy in a way.

He poured himself more champagne, leaned back with the cup, looked around the room without taking anything in. As if time had stopped, he thought, feeling that he had to make a decision. He had never felt so far away before, floating in the air above everything. He thought of those stories that describe death as a condition in which you can look down at the world from above. At some point the police would call; he had time to get things in order by then, he told himself.

He thought of Elisabeth and her brother, who was probably sitting in the living room with his legs spread wide at this very moment, lighting a cigarillo and making his usual remarks about Elisabeth's marriage. And as always she would have no reply to them, and later she would punish him, Jürgen, for it with even more contempt. What was it she had once said when they were going home in a taxi from a party at her boss's home? "How can you expect people to be interested in someone who spends almost all his time with dead Russians, can't talk about anything else, and hasn't the faintest notion of real life? What are they to talk to you about, how's there to be any bridge between you? If you were well known for your scholarship, appeared on TV and so on, then you could afford this sort of thing, but you're just a nonentity to them. And I'm sick and tired of having to explain you! Yes, my husband's work is rather boring, but you see, he's doing very important studies of Russian literature, he's kind of a genius in that field, so don't think that I of all people have ended up with the saddest sack in the place!"

The saddest sack in the place! That was how Elisabeth's brother had described him at their wedding.

Would he ever be so famous that her brother and everyone else would finally shut up? Famous enough for no one, not even he himself, to have to explain things anymore? Famous enough for Elisabeth to be proud of him?

The bank robber turned her head in her sleep, and her acne shone in the light from the ceiling lamps. Now she looked like any teenager asleep on the nearest chair after a class party. But that was deceptive! As he fixed his eyes on the bank robber, Jürgen's features hardened. How often she'd pointed the pistol at him in the course of the evening! She had even shoved it up against his forehead! And what had he been to her? A petty bourgeois, a coward! She hadn't been the faintest bit interested in his novel! She wasn't interested in anything but money. *"Know what a good hostage-taking story would be?"* To think he hadn't seen through her game! Instead he'd had movie-style fantasies, Bonnie and Clyde, like a sixteen-year-old! And all the time, stuffed to the eyeballs with pills, she'd probably have shot him the first chance she got!

Jürgen leaned back, breathing heavily. This was a life and death struggle, that was the way to look at it. Except that he hadn't struggled. He'd only wet his pants. The saddest sack in the place . . . *"But really I'm writing a novel." "I used to write stuff too . . ."*

And suddenly he saw himself as they would show him on TV: Jürgen Schröder, using his patience and courage to overpower the woman bank robber, the druggie. He saved himself, and supposing it had come to flight and a police chase he'd probably saved many other lives too, and he did it all alone. Here is our reporter at the scene of the crime, talking to Jürgen Schröder . . .

Jürgen raised the champagne bottle to his lips and emptied it. All was quiet except for the hum of the ceiling lights. He pictured his arrival in the living room at home. "Oh, is your brother still here? I hope you won't either of you mind if I just take a quick look at the news."

Herr Schröder, you were the last hostage, and you had to hold out for several hours in the bank alone with the hostage taker. In the end, and in dramatic circumstances, you managed to eliminate the bank robber.

Yes, but I'm really writing a novel.

When the phone rang—the police were calling at the agreed time—Jürgen was sitting well back in his chair, clutching the pistol in both hands, and staring at the bank robber as if hypnotized. At this moment, at the climax of his life-and-death struggle, he felt curiously numb. When the bank robber moved because the ringing of the phone woke her, he had to act. With his face half averted, he shot her four times, and then shouted for help.

THE RUDOLF FAMILY DOES
GOOD WORKS

"Herr Rudolf! Wait a minute." The caretaker's old wife straightened up, dropped her floorcloth into her bucket, and limped over to the stairs. Herr Rudolf stopped and removed his pom-pom hat. The snow on his shoes was melting. As a man with both a social conscience and a vague and confused attitude to professional cleaning ladies, he felt very ill at ease to see the puddle forming around his feet.

"Good day, Frau Simmes." Herr Rudolf tried to smile.

"Good day." The caretaker's wife dried her hands on her apron as she scrutinized the weedy little mathematics teacher without embarrassment. She didn't like him. Even when he moved in she had taken offense at his reproachful tone when he complained that the apartment building didn't have its own container for recycling glass, and every morning one of the daily papers described by her husband as liberal guff was sticking out of his letterbox.

"What is it, Frau Simmes?"

The old lady smoothed her apron, folded her arms, and asked triumphantly, "I suppose you know lodgers are forbidden in this building?"

Herr Rudolf felt his heart sink. "Yes, of course." And added with assumed surprise, "Why ask?"

"Because there's been a gentleman going in and out of your place for months."

"Oh, you must mean . . ."

"I mean the gentleman with the blue coat."

"But my dear Frau Simmes . . . !" Herr Rudolf acted as if he could hardly suppress his mirth. "That's my uncle. He's only visiting."

"Oh, your uncle, is he? So how come your uncle doesn't speak any German?"

"He's an ethnic German from Russia."

The old lady didn't seem able to make much of this reply, and Herr Rudolf was quick to explain. "You know what I mean, the Germans who were dragged off to Siberia by Stalin, or even worse were in concentration camps. He lost his parents when he was fifteen, and forgot the language entirely."

The caretaker's wife still looked skeptical. "He even forgot how to say 'Good day'?"

Herr Rudolf smiled sadly. "No, that's because he's scared. If every German word you speak has meant the danger of imprisonment for almost fifty years . . . well, you don't shake the habit off just like that."

The place smelled of food, and the sound of chattering voices came from the kitchen. Herr Rudolf hung up his coat on the rack and looked in the mirror to tidy his hair, which was sparse, but to make up for that he grew it long. He knew they made fun of his hairstyle in school, but he didn't mind anymore. He had resigned himself to the fact that his qualities were on the intellectual plane, and he cultivated the eccentric appearance of an artist. Sometimes he wrote articles for specialist mathematical journals, but his great love was poetry. He wrote it in secret: serious verse about life and the essence of humanity, as well as humorous squibs on politics and everyday life. He was planning to publish his poems some day, and often imagined the ecstatic welcome they would receive from literary critics.

When Herr Rudolf entered the kitchen his wife was just cutting a loin of veal into thin slices. She greeted him with a lackluster "Hello."

"Hello."

Chinese porcelain dishes containing various sauces stood on the dining table, along with a Sterno can and three place settings for a fondue. The radio was on. A pastor was saying what a good thing the November Revolution of 1989 in Germany had been. Herr Rudolf put his hands in his trouser pockets and watched his wife arranging the meat on a platter. Herr Olschewski had been living with them for the last nine months. At their first conversation he had said he was an emigrant from Kazakhstan. He paid his rent punctually, hardly ever put in an appearance, and left no mess behind him in the bathroom. Beyond that the Rudolfs took no interest in him. As a Russian of ethnic German origin he did not belong to their own cultural area, nor was he exotic; he seemed too different for them to get to know him more closely, and too like them to be boasted of as something special. Once Frau Rudolf had sighed, "If only he were Jewish!" For Herr and Frau Rudolf belonged to that section of the German population that liked to proclaim themselves friends and admirers of the Jewish people. However, the Rudolfs didn't personally know any Jews. So a Jewish lodger would have enriched their lives twice over.

Frau Rudolf suddenly turned and asked, "Anything wrong?"

Herr Rudolf shook his head. "No, it's just that . . ." And he tightened his lips. His wife rolled her eyes and turned to the stove. She had been familiar with this hesitant, indecisive attitude of his, seeing problems everywhere, for the last seventeen years. For twelve of those years she had considered it cowardly, for the rest she had thought it stupid.

". . . Frau Simmes asked me if Herr Olschewski was our lodger."

"So what did you say?"

"I said he was my uncle from Russia on a visit."

Frau Rudolf tasted the broth, put the spoon in the sink, and turned down the burner on the stove. Then she looked at the kitchen clock. "Where's Cornelia this time? Ever since she reached puberty . . ."

"Jutta!"

"What?"

"If they find out that he isn't my uncle we'll lose the apartment."

"Why would they find out?"

"Frau Simmes could tell the housing authorities—or ask Cornelia questions, and in her scatterbrained way Cornelia will let it all out."

"Cornelia will let nothing out in any scatterbrained way. She takes after me."

"Jutta, please!" Herr Rudolf raised his arms. "Our apartment is at stake! Our whole way of life!"

"Oh, well, if that's all . . ."

Frau Rudolf looked briefly at her husband, hoping he might laugh, or lose his temper, or something, anything. But he didn't understand, or anyway pretended not to. He slowly went over to the window, looking past the straw stars made by his daughter and out into the snow-covered street. Until a year ago his wife had gone to pottery classes at the adult education center. Then four months' work—Medea and her victims life-size, in thirty-six separate pieces—had exploded in the kiln, and she had thrown it all away. She's been getting more and more difficult every day since then, thought Herr Rudolf, although I'd be happy to help her find a new interest. If only she'd at least take up some kind of exercise.

Finally he gave himself a shake and announced, "I'll tell Herr Olschewski this evening that he must leave at the end of the month."

"You'll do no such thing! Do you know what Olschewski has brought us to date?" Frau Rudolf pointed to a set of Japanese stainless steel kitchen knives. "There!" Then she tapped the espresso machine. "Here!" And finally she flung open the kitchen cupboard, making the Rosenthal coffee service clink. "And here! Not to mention our vacation in Crete. Do you want us to go back to scrimping and saving?"

Herr Rudolf opened his mouth, looking pained, only to close it again with a sigh. Then the telephone in the corridor rang.

The kitchen door slammed, and Herr Rudolf heard his wife pick up the receiver.

"Rudolf here."

"Good day, Frau Rudolf. My name is Neuacher. I am calling on behalf of the Local Initiative Office for the Integration of Aid to Emigrants. In the context of our project 'A Bowl of Soup for Hermann—Germans Extend a Helping Hand to Ethnic Germans' it has come to our notice that Herr Ernst Olschewski, a Russian of German origin, is staying with you. Would you be prepared to answer a few questions about him?"

For a moment Frau Rudolf listened, speechless, to the humming on the line, and then replied coolly, "Go ahead."

"Does Herr Olschewski pay you rent?"

Frau Rudolf didn't stop to think long about that. "Of course not." There was a note of indignation in her voice.

The woman at the other end of the line uttered a cry of delight. "So there are still some people around with a sense of responsibility, ready to share their bread with others! Congratulations, Frau Rudolf. Would you tell me how long Herr Olschewski has been living with you?"

"Eleven months."

"Wonderful! Please hold the line."

Frau Rudolf could just hear voices at the other end of the receiver. "Eleven? . . . Then they're in the lead! . . . Any more names on the list? . . . No."

"Frau Rudolf?"

"Yes?"

"I am happy to tell you that you have won the Good Citizens Prize in our project 'A Bowl of Soup for Hermann.' For the next year you will receive a thousand Deutschmarks a month for special services to maintaining ethnic German awareness."

"But how could they know?" Herr Rudolf looked up from his empty plate. The news had quite taken his appetite away. Not only did the Olschewski problem now assume unexpected dimensions, he wanted nothing to do with a prize which, he correctly suspected, was awarded by people of strictly reactionary views. He hated any kind of patriotic-sounding German sentiments, unless they applied to saving local woods and meadows. He voted Social Democrat and was a paid-up member of the Mathematics Teachers for

Europe organization. "Or do we know anyone who's in contact with that sort of association?"

"Not us, but maybe Olschewski does," said Cornelia, taking a skewerful of meat out of the broth.

"Never mind how they know. The question is whether anyone's told Olschewski about this prize." Frau Rudolf helped herself to a spoonful of sauce and handed the dish to her daughter. Her face was flushed. The prospect of the money had exhilarated her. "If it comes out that he's paying rent we can wave good-bye to those twelve thousand marks."

Herr Rudolf said, "Let me remind you that if anyone finds out Olschewski's our lodger we'll be given notice to leave."

"Exactly. All the better about the prize. That makes it official: he's been living here for free. The one person who can endanger us is Olschewski himself. It'll be better if he doesn't go to the award ceremony."

Herr Rudolf was left speechless for a moment. "Jutta . . ."
"Yes?"

"Suppose I don't go either?"

Frau Rudolf cast him a scathing glance. "You are most certainly coming!"

When Herr Olschewski came home at seven-thirty, as he did every evening, Frau Rudolf was lying in wait for him. Olschewski was in his mid-forties, tall, fit, always clean-shaven and correctly dressed. He could have been a salesman of gentleman's fashions or a bank clerk. On their first meeting he had said he was doing a year's course with Federal German Mail, which was training former Russian postal officials to be German postal officials. What he really did, only Olschewski himself knew.

Frau Rudolf now struck up a conversation with him about the various associations for emigrants and exiles. He obviously had no idea about the prize, and she made him promise to tell outsiders in the future that he wasn't paying rent. The reason—"trouble with the management"—immediately sounded convincing to Herr Olschewski. However, had he known that he personally was the occasion for a public award ceremony, he would have moved out that very night.

Frau Rudolf told her husband about the conversation, and said, "His German's not so bad anyway."

"Just so long as it's not good enough for him to read the daily papers."

"Don't start on about that again. If he does happen to hear about the prize I'll fix it. Didn't you say yourself, better for us to get it than some right-wing vermin?"

A week later the Rudolf family were in the Volga Cellar as guests of honor at the award ceremony. The place was sold out. Frau Rudolf had told the organizers that Herr Olschewski had to stay at home because he had a bad attack of flu. There was great agitation. They'd been counting on a speech of thanks from Olschewski to his benefactors. The program had to be changed, and the organizers wondered whether everything was all aboveboard. But their wish to present a successful evening soon made them forget their doubts.

Herr Rudolf was wearing a beige corduroy suit, his wife had bought a brightly colored jacket and skirt for the occasion, and Cornelia was tugging unhappily at an embroidered blouse belonging to her mother. Her hair was in braids. Frau Rudolf had brought all this about by announcing that while it was not in the family's style to curry favor, they were getting too much money from these crazy folks not to go along with their ideas of how Germans ought to look, at least for one evening. A group in the folk costume of the Transylvanian Alps danced on stage to the sound of choral singing from the band, and Czech beer was served at the bar. The guests' faces were flushed. Many had rolled up their sleeves and were swaying in time to the music. When the dancing was over a young man in a smart blue, sparkly suit came up on stage, got behind a lectern, and began his speech with the words: "Ladies and gentlemen, dear children, dear friends, comrades, patriots, fellow countrymen—Germans!"

There was applause. Herr Rudolf took a deep breath. His wife assumed the outward appearance of someone entirely uninvolved. Cornelia ostentatiously sipped her apple juice.

". . . And now let's come to the real subject of this evening: the true victims of the Second World War. People who have lived a life of squalor and misery for forty-five years, a life of servitude and starvation, in exile and sickness—millions of German men, women, and children, from Dessau to Siberia!"

After further vigorous applause, the young man went on, "Some will say: but the Wall fell a year ago, and with it all the Communist terror regimes except for the Russian government, and that too will collapse sooner or later. To which I can only reply: the ghost of Communism may be banished, but—and I cannot emphasize this too strongly—the ghost of democracy has taken its place. For if we look at present conditions in Russia, Romania, the whole of Eastern Europe, where German people are starving and international gangsters rule, it can truly be described only as a ghost!"

The applause for this was relatively sparse, denoting not so much disagreement as the confusion of the majority of the guests as they worked it out about all those ghosts. The speaker noticed, and was quick to add, "What we Germans need is not democracy, we need potatoes!"

Everyone had now picked up the thread again, and the sound of shouts and stamping feet rose to a tempestuous roar. Suddenly Herr Rudolf turned to his wife and muttered, "I can't stand this! I'll have something to say about it, oh, won't I just! And it's all your fault. I never wanted to come!"

Frau Rudolf could not hear exactly what he was saying, and thought he was simply finding fault as usual.

Soon after that the speech was over, and an elderly lady of important appearance came on stage to ask this year's winners of the Good Citizens Prize to come up and receive it.

". . . the Rudolf family who have self-sacrificingly endeavored to give a new start in life to an emigrant, Herr Ernst Olschewski, who unfortunately could not come tonight because of sickness. A round of applause, please!"

As he stood up Herr Rudolf knocked a glass over, and in apologizing he noticed how his voice trembled. He had spent the last few minutes planning a short speech to say how "distasteful, almost Fascist" he considered the address that had just been given, and declining the prize on the grounds of his moral and democratic principles.

Herr Rudolf, his wife, and Cornelia went up on stage. First the prize was handed over. A symbolic, outsized check for twelve thousand D-marks, and a hand-embroidered wall hanging showing Germany with its 1937 frontiers. Hands were shaken, cheers rang out. Then the lady of important appearance asked Herr Rudolf to say a few words. He went to the lectern and cleared his throat, but suddenly his eye fell on Cornelia, and he stopped short. She was his only child; she had her life all before her. How will the audience react, thought Herr Rudolf suddenly, if I say my piece? Will there be a scuffle? Or will we be blacklisted, and then Cornelia can never go to school with an easy mind again? You read about such things in the papers all the time: neo-Nazis, threatening letters, bombs . . .

After Herr Rudolf had said a few words thanking the organizers for the prize, he and his family went back to their seats, and a Silesian songwriter came on stage. Soon after that the Rudolf family left the Volga Cellar to the sound of the refrain: "In Breslau stands a little tree, growing juicy plums for me."

As his wife drove the car home through the evening traffic, and Cornelia undid her braids in the back, Herr Rudolf, in the passenger seat, was making up for the speech he had not delivered out of his sense of paternal responsibility. He argued against the occasion they had just attended, he denounced it, he gesticulated and thundered against it with such fervor that his wife kept glancing at him in surprise. It was a long time since she'd seen him so sure of himself. He spoke of foreigners and tolerance, of living side by side or in a real community, of civilization and the equal status of all cultures, of a world without borders and without wars, of human beings who saw themselves first and foremost as inhabitants of Planet Earth, not the representatives of some tribe or some piece of land. He carried on like this until his wife had found a place to park. Herr Rudolf got out of the car feeling that he could keep the check, and that for now anyway he had saved his ethics intact.

Once in their apartment, they decided to invite Herr Olschewski to a lavish supper. Cornelia was sent to bed.

Frau Rudolf saw this supper as one of the things she had planned in order to give the unsuspecting Herr Olschewski what she estimated to be a proper share in the prize money. In the future she would do his laundry, and cook for him in the evening, and she'd sometimes take him into town in the car. She also hoped to relieve her husband's guilty conscience in this way.

Herr Olschewski looked up in surprise when his land-lady entered his room after ten in the evening. He was sitting on his bed in pajamas, reading a book. He was even more surprised when she asked him to come into the living room for a glass of wine and some supper. When he first moved in, it had been explained that apart from the bathroom and the kitchen, the rest of the apartment was out of bounds to him. He thanked her politely and said, in heavily accented German, that he would just get dressed and then join them.

"No, no, do stay in your pajamas," said Frau Rudolf. "We don't stand on ceremony."

In the living room Herr Rudolf was setting out a buffet supper of gooseliver pâté, salmon, and other delicacies, along with two expensive bottles of white wine. He was whistling to himself as he did so, in high spirits, as if he had just passed an exam. The three of them drank to "our future life together." Over supper, the reunification of Germany was discussed. Herr Rudolf thought it necessary but too soon just now, and finally it gave them another reason to drink a toast. Herr Olschewski agreed to everything Herr Rudolf said, but otherwise confined himself to praising the food. Herr and Frau Rudolf were both soon sure that they were dealing with a totally unpolitical and uneducated person, and went on to ask their guest to tell them some Russian toasts. They repeated these with the wrong emphasis, which occasioned them great amusement.

After they had wished each other good night, and Herr Olschewski had gone back to his room, the phone rang. Herr Rudolf picked it up. A male voice announced, "My name is Beppo. You have me to thank for that prize. I gave your names to the association. Must have been a nasty shock for Olschewski or whatever he's calling himself these days. No wonder he stayed at home. Flu, was it?" The caller laughed. "Well, tell him hello from me, and you can say I'm not the only one who knows where he is, so he'd better think my proposition over again. If we don't inform on the others, then they will inform on us."

Half an hour later Herr Rudolf, sitting at the kitchen table, was repeating for the umpteenth time, "What the hell have we got mixed up in?"

"If only you wouldn't be so pessimistic for once." His wife was sitting opposite him. It was long past midnight. "What could happen to us? If Olschewski is really up to no good we'll throw him out. Then it won't matter if he hears about the prize or not. You just wait, it will all turn out okay."

Next morning the doorbell rang at seven. Herr Rudolf, who was in the bathroom, jumped with fright. His nerves were all on edge. He had woken up in the middle of the night and couldn't get to sleep again for thinking and worrying about Olschewski. What would happen if Olschewski was a criminal? Or even worse, how was he, Herr Rudolf, to behave if he wasn't? Wouldn't they have to let him live here for free from now on? Would his wife give back the prize money? She'd said she might start up a small pottery studio with it—would giving up that idea mean the end of their marriage?

When Herr Rudolf opened the door and saw three police officers outside, the apartment building's management was the first thing to come to mind. He broke into a sweat. He already saw himself in jail and his family without a roof over their heads.

"Good morning. Does a man called Rainer Fritsch, alias Ernst Olschewski, live with you?"

"Why?"

One of the officers took a piece of paper out of his pocket. "We have a warrant for his arrest."

Herr Rudolf breathed again. So it was only about Olschewski! The police would take him away, and that would be the end of it once and for all! He was so relieved that he didn't even ask what the warrant was for. He took the policemen straight to Olschewski's room. They went in and came out a little later, with Olschewski in handcuffs. Yesterday evening's naïve, unassuming lodger had become a figure commanding respect, a man with stern features and a cool gaze. He looked briefly at Herr and Frau Rudolf, who were standing in the corridor, petrified, and said, in faultless German, "Thank you very much for the accommodation." Two of the officers led him out of the apartment. The third asked, "Was it you who made the anonymous phone call?"

Yet again, Frau Rudolf's instinct for the answers that people wanted to hear came to her aid, and she replied,

"Well, that depends. If he really broke the law, maybe. But we're not informers."

The officer smiled and nodded, satisfied. "Don't worry, your name won't be made public. But you did very well to let us know of your suspicions. Until the Wall came down, Rainer Fritsch was a Stasi officer. In the espionage department."

"Good God!" Herr Rudolf looked stunned. To him, and many others, the Stasi had been the very quintessence of evil since the Wall came down, an organization comparable to the Gestapo or the South American death squads.

The policeman frowned. "But your suspicions, as expressed on the phone, did nudge us in that direction?"

Herr Rudolf looked at his wife. Without any hesitation, she said, "Yes, indeed, but they were only suspicions."

"Hm." The policeman seemed doubtful. All the same, he said, "Well, there was a ten-thousand-marks reward for information leading to Fritsch's arrest. That'll be payable to you, then."

He left, and the door closed behind him. Herr and Frau Rudolf looked at each other. They couldn't believe what had just happened until they had fallen into one another's arms, kissing as they hadn't kissed for years.

Herr Rudolf whispered, "You were splendid!" And his wife said, "Well, one couldn't have the caller getting a reward. There's nothing worse than an informer."

Herr Rudolf phoned the high school and said he was sick. Around midday he withdrew from his wife's arms, rose from the bed, and got dressed. They had been making plans for what to do with the various sums of money, and agreed that their life together must be different and better in the future. But all the same, much should stay as it was.

That evening Herr Rudolf came back from the civic reception center for Russian Jewish emigrants. He had a young man with him. Frau Simmes met them on the stairs. The caretaker's wife apologized for her suspicions about the lodger. She'd read about the Good Citizens Prize in the paper, she said, and was proud to live in the same building as the Rudolfs.

In the living room, Herr Rudolf introduced the young man to his wife. "Herr Walentin Rosen."

"Does he speak German?"

"Not much."

"Did you explain that he'll have to pay only half the usual rent?"

"Yes, of course. And that he must say he isn't paying any at all."

Herr Rosen wasn't following a word of this. His new landlady beamed at him and said, "Shalom!" Then she kissed her husband on the forehead. "I'm going to call the Hasselbergs and invite them to a meal. Georg was reading the Talmud on vacation, and Almut will be just bursting with envy anyway."

Herr Rudolf watched his wife go. She looked ten years younger. Then he looked at Herr Rosen. He was still wearing his coat, standing around awkwardly.

Perhaps I'll even let the management know about you officially, thought Herr Rudolf. They can get to know what I'm like! And we'll go to the Jewish community and other organizations. No one's going to take *you* away from us!

AT PEACE

Almost everyone in the village liked the old man from the city; no one knew him really well. Years ago, when he first came driving along the main road in his big, dark blue Citroën, which appeared to the villagers more like a fish than a car, on his way to look at the once magnificent but now dilapidated manor house on the edge of the woods, the local inhabitants thought he was one of the usual fools who had seen the FOR SALE ads in some real estate brochure, saw the flattering photograph, and thereupon imagined living like one of the landed gentry during their summer vacations. But when they had actually seen the place, spent an hour stumbling over rubble and putting their feet through rotten floorboards, when their jackets were dirty with crumbling plaster and cobwebs, and the wind blowing through empty window frames and holes in the walls and the roof had made them shiver, all they wanted was to go home to their city apartments with nice white walls and central heating. However, Herr Kanter, who was then in his mid-sixties but had a full head of white hair and looked like a fit fifty-year-old, was different. Matti, who held the key to the manor house and was paid a hundred marks a month by the joint heirs to show potential buyers around, said in the inn later that Kanter had been making notes the whole time, unimpressed by the stage of the property, and that finally, when they left the manor, he, Kanter, could say almost to the nearest Deutschmark just what renovation would cost. A week later he came back, walked through the village, had a couple of glasses of schnapps at the bar in the inn, and talked to the villagers about the weather and the agricultural produce grown here. Summer came earlier and lasted longer on the southwest border of the plain of the Rhine than anywhere else in Germany; besides vineyards and almost every kind of fruit the local farmers also raised pigs and cattle, and there was a chicken farm too. Work on the renovation began next month, and when the first wing of the manor house was inhabitable, three furniture vans arrived and Kanter moved in. Word had gone around that he had something to do with the stock exchange, and since his business was conducted almost entirely by telephone and computer, he could do it just as well here as in the city. He was rich, or at least better off than anyone else in the village and probably the entire district, you only had to look at all the expense he went to, even getting the door to the old cowshed with its woodcarvings and metal fittings restored down to the smallest detail. However, hardly anyone in the village felt envious, for he was rich as naturally as other folks are naturally blond or dark. He did not make a great display of his money, nor did he keep it a secret. When the farmers complained of their financial troubles in the bar, waxing indignant about the European Community, taxes, and new regulations banning drugs in animal feed and thus restricting growth and yield, he never pretended to be one of them himself, however distantly. Instead, the longer he lived in the village the more often he gave the locals tips on how to invest any spare cash they might have for a while, and after a few years he began providing financial backing for various projects that he thought would be successful, such as organically reared pork and a new automatic bottling plant.

"Tell me, Kanter, you buy my wife's jam, I was just thinking we could make a business of it. Nothing big, we don't have a huge crop of apricots, but to sell to folks who want something special and don't mind about the price. Not here, of course. Do you think there are shops in town that would be interested in a kind of gourmet jam like that?"

"Yes, indeed. But tell your wife to go easy on the sugar; the last few jars were too sweet for me. And if you're thinking of selling the jam professionally, then the sugar content has to be on the label, and the lower it is the better for an exclusive clientele."

That same afternoon Kanter called a high-class delicatessen that he knew from the old days, and the next year the jam business was well under way. But when the farmer invited Kanter to a roast lamb dinner by way of thanks, Kanter declined in a friendly manner. It was always the same: you could talk to him and drink with him in the bar, you could chat with him in the street, and on his daily walk across the fields he even seemed to like company for part of the way, but he would never visit anyone's home. He never invited anyone to the manor house either. Even when he needed craftsmen he brought them in from outside. That had caused a good deal of indignation at first, since the local craftsmen had thought they were sure of jobs for the next few years. But when Kanter kept paying first the plumber, then the electrician, and then the builder under the table for a few weeks' work in town, indignation gave way to gratitude. People wondered about Kanter's convoluted methods, but soon put them down to the eccentricity expected of city folk in general. It struck only a few that strangers were always strangers, however they behaved, but usually went to some pains to make friends with the locals, as if trying to curry favor, while Kanter was obviously extremely keen to remain a stranger. The only villagers he allowed on his premises were two farmers who delivered him potatoes, apples, and wine, but they never saw any more than the drive from the front gate to the house and the cellar where provisions were stored. Which did not prevent them from bragging to other people, independently of each other, about the magnificent, luxurious rooms through which Kanter always escorted them, complete with golden fitted kitchens and television sets the size of cars.

And then there was Schuster. Some thought him what you might call the black sheep of the village, a disgrace to the locality; to others he was a poor unlucky devil to be pitied. Only four years ago a strong young man with his own vineyard inherited from his father, and presumably a secure future, after his wife's death he had begun drinking and taking any other substances he could obtain and afford. Falling further and further into addiction and dissipation, he had sold first the vineyard and then his house at knock-down prices, and after that he slept in a hut in the woods. He drew social security, which he drank and smoked away, washed in the stream if he washed at all, wore clothes given to him now and then by friends from the old days and relatives, and ate at his aunt's. In return for enduring her reproachful silence, he got a hot meal every day at noon. Sometimes he roamed the streets by night, wailing or bawling indistinctly, and landed up in the police station again the next morning.

So it was a minor miracle, and no one knew just how it had begun, when at some point it became usual to see Schuster going in and out of Kanter's place. The first to notice was the wife of an insurance rep. She was just coming back from a walk when she saw Schuster wobbling down the road to the manor house on his rusty old bike. She stopped, saw him put the bike down on the grass by the door, and was about to go after him, supposing that he had some stupid plan in mind—the woman felt responsible, for Schuster was part of the village community, even if on its outer margin—when he pressed the bell, said something to the intercom, and the door opened for him. The woman waited twenty minutes or so for Schuster to come out, and then went home as fast as she could. From home she phoned the local policeman, told him what had happened, and together they tried to find an explanation, fearing the worst all the time. Had Schuster wangled his way into the manor house under a false name in one of his few lucid moments, to steal the golden doors from the fitted kitchen? And if so, what had he done with Kanter? Tied him up? Even killed him? After all, in spite of his robust appearance, Kanter was an old man and not as strong as an even partially sober Schuster. And wasn't the splendidly renovated manor house that Schuster passed every day on the way to his hut bound to remind him, every time he saw it, of the wretchedness of his own life? It was even possible that he wanted to harm Kanter out of sheer envy. And then perhaps he'd set the manor house on fire. Automatically, both callers went to the windows looking toward the woods with their phones, to see if any smoke was rising to the sky. Finally the policeman decided that before they took any other steps to rescue Kanter he should phone him first, not least because in spite of the possibility of a crime on Kanter's property he was afraid to set foot there. He hung up and then called Kanter's number. When Kanter answered, the policeman heaved a sigh of relief.

"Aren't you feeling well?" asked Kanter.

"I'm fine, we were just anxious about you."

"I beg your pardon?"

Laboriously, and leaving out several details, which in retrospect appeared hysterical, the policeman mentioned what the woman had seen, and said they'd been wondering if there was anything sinister about Schuster's entering Kanter's property.

"He's working for me," explained Kanter.

"Really? Oh. Well . . . you do know Schuster isn't always . . . let's say entirely responsible for his actions?"

"In my employment he's getting just enough to keep his alcohol level up but leave him able to work."

"Hm. Well, if that's it . . . you see, he isn't really a bad fellow, but ever since his wife died . . . they'd only been married a few months when she went under the truck."

"People can always find reasons for drinking."

"How do you mean?"

"If she hadn't been run over, maybe *she* would have provided the reasons."

His cool tone took the policeman aback. It sounded almost as if Kanter disliked Schuster. But then why give him a job? When he had hung up the policeman realized that, for the first time, he felt he didn't like Kanter.

Over the following weeks a number of others began to share the police officer's feeling about Kanter's attitude to Schuster. They were seen together more and more frequently—when Schuster was helping Kanter do the shopping, or driving him somewhere in the car—but the way Kanter treated Schuster, in public too, made most people feel that Schuster would be better off if he still spent his time sitting in the sun with a bottle of wine.

"Once an alcoholic always an alcoholic!" snapped Kanter at the filling station when Schuster spilled a little oil because his hands were trembling. Or in the baker's, which was cramped and where the air was hot from the baker's oven, he would snarl, "My God, I wish you'd wash properly for a change!" And when he was in the bar on his own, he made fun of Schuster to other people. "You should see how long it takes him to get once across the garden with a wheelbarrow! Weaving this way and that! It's a wonder there are any flowers left standing!"

Before a month was up Kanter's public reputation was ruined, for the time being anyway. In the end, people said to themselves, and after putting on a pretense for a while, he had turned out to be exactly what you might expect of an arrogant townie.

But hardly another month later, the picture had changed again. Schuster was now living at the manor house with Kanter, his clothes were clean, he rode a moped, and he had stopped drinking, which meant that his wailing and bawling in public had stopped too. In fact he made not a sound, said the bare minimum when he was out shopping, and returned only a brief reply when anyone greeted him. Only one thing was the same, was perhaps even worse than before, and that was the sadness in his eyes. One of the farmers delivering potatoes to Kanter said he had heard Kanter, through the open window, telling Schuster, for what was obviously the ump-teenth time, that he mustn't try denying his pain. The longer Schuster stayed on the wagon the more depressed he seemed to be, and although no one would admit it, he had been much less disruptive to the daily life of the village as an ordinary nuisance than as grief personified. He visited his wife's grave every evening, and you sometimes saw him at the road junction where the accident had happened—places he had not gone near before. People avoided him in the street more and more frequently, for fear of the way he looked, and their feeling that they could do nothing to relieve it.

At the same time what were soon being ironically called "Kanter's visitors" began to arrive. First it was an elderly lady in a taxi. She wore a sparkly suit, a pearl necklace, sunglasses, and all who met her in the village wondered when they'd seen her on television. She grandly ordered an espresso in the bar, and when there wasn't any she asked for a still mineral water, but the landlord couldn't provide that either, so in the end she settled for a roll of mints.

"Very well. Now please tell me where Kanter lives!"

The landlord was surprised by the fury in her voice, and since by now Kanter was, in a way, part of the village, he hesitated to reply. He carefully wiped the beer taps before he asked, "Why?"

"Why?" she barked back, and the landlord had a feeling that the lady, or whatever this volcano should properly be called, would have liked to spit her mint in his face.

"Yes, why?" he repeated calmly. "Herr Kanter doesn't like to be bothered."

"Dear me, how touching! Are you part of some kind of royal court he has?"

"I don't know what you mean by that, but I'm no public address book, that's for sure."

It took the lady a moment to absorb this, and then she said, in chilly tones, "Kanter simply disappeared two years ago without so much as saying good-bye to anyone. Not to our children, not to me, not to his best friends. We didn't do anything for a while, because he'd already gone off on his own quite often, but he always came back after a few months at the most. And now I discover that he's built up an entirely new life here." She paused and looked sharply at the landlord. "So would you kindly tell me where he lives?"

The landlord scratched his chin and looked thoughtfully at the lady. Of course they had often wondered why Kanter seemed to have neither family nor friends.

Finally he said, "If you go further down the street you'll see the place: it's the manor house just on the edge of the woods. All freshly painted, with a new roof."

The taxi had been waiting outside the door, and the landlord watched through the window as the lady got in and told the driver where to go. Several people said later that she spent all afternoon standing at Kanter's gate, ringing the bell and knocking. She came back to the inn late in the evening, took a room, and stayed for a week. She went to Kanter's house every day, but the gate stayed closed. Since no one answered the phone either, they would probably soon have broken in by force if Schuster, who came into and went out of the property by secret ways, had not said, in answer to questions, that Kanter was alive and in the best of health.

Soon after the lady had left, a positive bombardment of letters and telegrams began. Almost daily, the postmaster took down threatening, furious, and sometimes pleading messages over the line, which he passed on to Kanter and also imparted, under the seal of secrecy, to anyone who wanted to know what they said. Kanter was obviously one of a large family whose members were positively competing to see who would be first to drive or lure him out of hiding. The telegrams mentioned incurable diseases, financial disasters, and accidents, or they announced engagements and births. It got to the point where the postmaster and his wife wondered whether Kanter's sons and daughters were driving their cars into walls or having babies for the sole purpose of forcing their father to return. But none of it seemed to impress Kanter. Once, when he happened to be at the gate and took delivery of a telegram in person, he crumpled it up unread before the postmaster's eyes as they discussed the flood damage done by a storm the previous day.

Further visits followed, along similar lines: two men of Kanter's own age arrived and also took rooms in the inn, but soon gave up the pointless ringing and knocking at Kanter's gate, and devoted themselves instead to consuming the products of the local wine and spirits industry. They spent several days sitting on the patio of the inn, in the late summer sun, telling stories of the old days, laughing a lot and raising their glasses in the direction of Kanter's house. Next came a pretty young woman, who made vain attempts to climb the wall, which had iron spikes on top, and who then spent a whole weekend sitting on a deckchair outside Kanter's gate. She combined the hope of taking him by surprise as he left his property with the opportunity to get a nice tan. To that end she took off her blouse, and quite a number of farmers told their wives that, unusually for a Sunday, they had to go out to the fields to mend a fence or tend a sick cow. Finally a red convertible arrived with two couples who, having walked around Kanter's property for a while, went walking in the village and took photographs of its squares, walls, inhabitants, flowers, even wheelbarrows. They asked in the inn which chair Kanter normally chose, they photographed that too, as well as the landlord, the display of spirits behind the bar, and the view of the marketplace through the window. They said hardly anything, and when they did speak it was in a whisper. One of the men shed tears. The landlord felt sorry for them, and gave them a bottle of wine when they left, which made the man shed more tears, so that in the end the landlord was glad when the sad little company finally drove away again.

People did appear now and then after that, and having failed in the object of their journey usually drowned their sorrows at the inn, but the intervals between visits became longer, and a time came when they stopped altogether. Letters still kept coming for a while, and then it was only postcards for special occasions.

During the time when all these visitors came, Schuster went on going to see his wife's grave every evening. Apart from that he worked fourteen hours a day, said nothing at all now, and only a few jokers still greeted him in the street, deriving amusement from his dour expression.

But then spring came, and so did the day when Schuster entered the inn again for the first time in years. As if it were the most natural thing in the world, as if he didn't see the surprised faces around him, he went to the bar, signaled to the landlord, said: "A b-b-b . . . ," looked triumphantly around, and continued, "bar of chocolate and a mineral water, please!"

News of his presence at the inn soon got around the village, and as evening approached more and more people came to see it with their own eyes, feeling glad that Schuster was back, so to speak. There had indeed been indications that some such thing might happen, for he had been heard whistling these last few months, or had been seen joking with children, but no one had expected such a sudden and total change. As if a long forgotten switch on him had been pressed, his eyes had cleared, and anyone who didn't look and listen very carefully would have had the impression that he was talking and laughing as heartily and exuberantly as before the accident.

"Hey, Rütters," he said, turning to one of the farmers, "remember how you passed my hut in summer, and you said the stink of drugs would get everywhere and I'd give the whole village a bad reputation, when all I'd done was hang my socks out to air?"

Rütters looked up from his beer, and after the others had stopped laughing he said, "A joint like that would make me dizzy, anyway."

"As an old pothead you should know."

Rütters growled, "I was once young too."

"In the days when folks smoked unwashed socks."

While Schuster stuck to mineral water, and everyone else celebrated this new development by getting drunk, Kanter's absence was felt more and more strongly. No remark could be passed about Schuster's last few years, no joke could be cracked on the subject without someone in the room thinking of Kanter. Puzzling as his conduct to Schuster had often been, and although many still wondered what all that carping of his had been good for, it was obvious that he was responsible for the change in the man. But no one dared ask Schuster himself about him. There was a kind of mystery about the two men's relationship, although no one could have said what might be behind it. Only after midnight and many a glass of schnapps did one of the men pull himself together and ask, as if just incidentally, "Didn't I see Kanter drive into town today?"

Schuster said, in surprise, "No, he's at home. Why?"

"Oh, just wondering." The man shrugged. "He could have come in to drink a sparkling water with you."

Schuster did not reply, but you could see that he had been thinking something of the same kind himself. The subject was quickly changed.

The company went home late, and that evening was to serve as a subject of conversation in the village for a long time, not least because Schuster was the only one who woke up the next morning without a thick head.

A few weeks later Kanter had to go into the hospital. Schuster took him there, visited him every day, and took him fruit and newspapers. Kanter came home thin and hollow-cheeked. He walked unsteadily, and when he picked up a glass his hand trembled. Schuster had now found a small apartment of his own on the marketplace, but he still often spent the night at the manor house because of Kanter's condition. When Kanter was better they could be seen walking through the fields together, and visiting the inn, where they usually sat in silence over tea and sparkling water. Whether they were talking to each other, or joining in the conversation at the bar, it was soon clear that they had switched roles. Schuster led the conversation, cracked jokes, ordered drinks, and when Kanter spilled something told him to concentrate and try to get control of his weakened nerves and muscles by willpower, he mustn't let himself go. But Kanter hardly reacted. He sat back in his chair with an absent gaze, tugging at his stained trousers. Only when Schuster turned away from him, talked to other people or argued with them, for instance when he asked a farmer if he had ever seen a single one of the millions of Yugoslavians who, the farmer claimed, were coming to take his fields away from him, only then could Kanter sometimes be seen looking up with a bright gaze and smiling.

In the fall Kanter had to go into the hospital again, and once more Schuster supplied him with reading matter and vitamins. Kanter came home even thinner and shakier than before, and Schuster hardly left his side now. A basket case and an ex-alcoholic bound to him by gratitude, some said. Others thought they sensed a genuine mutual understanding between the two men that didn't need words. For you really heard Kanter and Schuster talk only of food and the weather, and then not at any length either.

But whether you were among those who explained the relationship as duty or those who thought it was friendship, no one could believe it when news emerged one day that Kanter had fired Schuster, both as his gardener and as a private individual. Schuster's landlady had been to the bakery in the morning, the baker's wife had told the postmaster, and by midday half the village knew. Of course, if Schuster had left because he was tired of nursing the old man . . . but what did this mean?

That evening at the inn rumors were rife: Schuster had stolen from Kanter—Kanter had changed his will in favor of Schuster, and Schuster had tried to poison him by giving him the wrong dose of his medication—Schuster had been too boastful, had been acting like the owner of the property already—in spite of all those women who'd come knocking at his door, maybe Kanter swung the other way and Schuster didn't fancy it. And so on. Like everyone else, Schuster was not allowed into the house now, and even outside the property you never saw the two of them together any more. Schuster avoided questions, or played down the incident as just getting fired in the normal way. But sometimes he couldn't help shaking his head despondently and admitting that he had no idea what had really happened. They'd been for a walk in the morning, laughing as they agreed that it was lucky Schuster had given up the booze, if only because Kanter would soon have to be pushed about in a wheelchair, and he didn't want to end up like the wheelbarrow that Schuster had once rammed hard into an iron girder when drunk.

". . . and at midday I made us some lunch, and then he lay down for a rest the same as usual. When the phone rang I picked it up quickly so it wouldn't wake him, because he has another handset by his bed, but he was on the line already. It was his doctor. So I hung up and went on tidying the kitchen. When he came down later he looked so strange, as if he had eaten something he didn't like. He didn't say a word for a long time, but that was nothing unusual. Recently he's often just sat there saying nothing, watching me work. He likes it when people work and you can see they know what they're doing, he told me once, never mind whether it's mixing cement or managing a company. So I repaired the ventilation over the stove, and oiled the hinges on the window shutters, and did something else, and he just sat there all the time. It must have been an hour passed like that, until he suddenly told me I must go. I still remember what I said— I mean, I was glad to hear him talking again. I said, sure, and what would you like me to get you while I'm out? Something to eat? Some plaster for repairs, something to plant in the garden? But no, none of that. He said I was to go away and never come back!"

A few weeks later Kanter had a demolition firm from the city destroy his house and grounds. The village was bewildered, and not a few thought Kanter ought to be committed. It was his place, of course, but didn't individuals have a responsibility to the community? Could a senile old man just destroy the showpiece of the village, even if it was he who had restored it to that status? But before the mayor and the police could step in and object, citing the preservation of ancient monuments, there was nothing left to preserve. Only one wing of the house was still standing, and amidst the ruins it looked like something left over from the Second World War. And to crown it all Kanter didn't even have the rubble cleared away. Anyone who went into the woods now had to pass a scene of carnage. Even the beautiful garden with its fruit trees, its hedges of berry fruits, and its rosebushes a hundred years old had not been spared; the bulldozer had smashed them all to matchwood.

The most idiotic, pointless thing of all, people thought later, was that Kanter was back in the hospital only a month later, and he died there. Pointless, assuming that Kanter had liked his house in its wrecked condition.

The situation left Schuster no peace, and as he really wanted to know what had been going on in Kanter's mind he went to the hospital to talk to the nurse who had looked after the old man during his last few days. In spite of the pain, Kanter had seemed calm, she told him.

". . . I once even said to him, 'You sometimes look really happy.' And he said, 'Not happy, but at peace.' He'd known about his sickness a long time, she said, and for the last few weeks he'd known he was about to die. But you see, he said, the only bad thing about death is having to leave behind so much that you've loved, and I've made sure there's nothing left that I'd mind parting with. They say even the wine isn't going to be good this year, he told me, too much rain, and he even laughed a little."

"Was that all he said?" asked Schuster.

"Well, he didn't say much more, only good morning and so on. Except that in the night just before he died, he rang for me, and I could see he wouldn't last much longer. He did have tears in his eyes after all, and he reached for my hand. He could only whisper now, and the last thing I heard, he said, 'It doesn't work,' and he asked if I could bring him something smelling of a garden. But when I came back with some flowers he was already dead."